A WALK BACK IN TIME

D. E. Legge

Published by PPR Publishing,
19 Kingswell Road, Northampton NN2 6QB

www.pprpublishing.co.uk

A CIP catalogue record for this book
is available from the British Library.

ISBN: 978 1 0685176 6 2

CONTENTS

1170 Bishop Becket

I am a poor woman of Canterbury and I can neither read nor write. Giles the scrivener tells me he takes my words down true so I must believe him. Giles' mother is English but he is the youngest son of a Norman esquire so can write in the French and Latin. English is not the language that is writ. Even after a hundred years the money and learning is all with the Normans. God will judge them.

I pray that God will likewise judge the wickedness of all men, the greatest most. Our Lady was the wife of a carpenter they tell me, but it makes it no easier to be poor and a woman. I am old, and remember the sufferings of the common folk when anarchy reigned. The sheriffs and reeves took coin to bend the law. When I was a maid they said that the soldiers who came and fought for the empress Mathilda had the right of it. I know not if this were the truth, but all the soldiers did bad things and stole and burned and worse. Then came King Henry and justice was done and the castles of the wicked were pulled down and new sheriffs were sworn. It was never so well though, if you were a woman. The priests say it is the curse of Eve.

Father Edward Grimm hath put down in Latin what happened that night; the twenty ninth of December in the sixteenth year of King Henry. I was there but he did not write of me. I clean God's house, though I cannot go into the sanctuary nor touch the reliquaries. To clean the spoor of the rats who gnaw the tallow in the cressets, or get rid of stray dogs and their mess, I *can* do. That night as the sun was setting I came to the door to go down into the crypt and sweep it. The brothers hear vespers there, but Our Lord's body not being present on the altar I might go in. Four men in brown cloaks had gathered outside by a tree. It was bitter cold and the ground was white with ice. No one lingered except perhaps the uttermost poor, and even they would have found sanctuary on such an eve. The light was waning, but praise God, my eyesight is still good. Their cloaks were plain, but they had boots of fine Cordova leather. They moved toward the Minster, but left a bundle beneath the tree. It was a hempen bag and I opened it. Four swords, small swords with curved cutting blades. They are called falchions. I knew from the talk at the time of the anarchy when death was in every man's mouth, that they were for close work; stabbing, butchery.

Should I take up the knives and run? As I thought on this, the men came back and I hurried into the church. I looked back and the men were following. The brothers were singing their office as they processed down the aisle toward the stairs to the crypt. I approached a brother but he ignored me. I caught hold of his habit and held it tight. He looked down with a look of disgust, pulled me from him and kicked me with his foot. A priest once told me that it is writ in Scripture that a sick woman held the hem of Our Lord's garment and he was not displeased but was gentle with her. I was upon the floor. As Bishop Thomas led the monks into the crypt, I saw the four men follow them. I cared not if a woman must keep silent. I thought on Our Lord and our Blessed Lady and I called out,

"Ware! Ware! Men carrying knives follow you!'
I ran towards the stairs to be met by brothers running away toward the west door shouting for help. I did not run away but went down the steps into the crypt. The great wax

candles on the altar steps gave light. I could see four men holding Bishop Thomas at the steps to the altar; with them no one but father Edwin.

One of the murderers cried, "Absolve and restore those you have excommunicated!"

Bishop Thomas' voice was strong as he replied, "They have not repented. I will not absolve."

Then the men laid hands on Thomas, and would have pulled him out of the crypt, but Edwin held onto him, and I ran forward and grabbed the bishop's robes also.

Then I saw those wicked knives bright in the candlelight uplift and Bishop Thomas said clearly, "I am ready to die, but hurt not my people neither lay nor clerk."

Then then the knives came down and they stabbed the bishop many times, but he did not die and recognising one of the knights cried, "Touch me not, Reginald, you owe me fealty and subjection."

To which the man replied, "No faith nor subjection do I owe you, against my fealty to the king."

With this, the wicked man took his sword and cut off the top of the Bishop's head and his blood flowed freely all around us.

Bishop Thomas lay dead and father Edwin was wounded sore in the arm. I took off my linen head-cloth and bound his arm with it. The murderers had fled and soon the crypt was filled with people who took away the body and gave succour to Edwin.

I asked one of the monks if I should help to clean the crypt but he replied, "This blood is the blood of a holy martyr and only the brothers must touch it now."

They tell me that those murderous knights were not punished for their crime. Their lands were not even forfeit. They went to the pope, who said their sin would be absolved if they made pilgrimage to the Holy Land. Is it not strange that their penance was so light for so monstrous a crime, while a poor man will be whipped if he steals so much as a coney to feed his family, and hanged if he taketh a deer or a sheep?

It is now three years since that terrible eve and Bishop Thomas has been made a saint by pope Alexander. Already the pilgrims come and people grow rich selling relics. I have my bloody apron still from that night. If the monks knew I kept it, they would take it, cut and sell it in little pieces, but I keep it. Poor and old as I am, when laid in my tomb, my body will be wrapped in linen cloth, stained with the blood of a holy martyr.

1291 Playing by the Rules

A story of the Albigensian heretics who called themselves 'The Good Christians'

My name is Claude Anne Perrot and I am of a great age. I have nigh on four score years, being born one thousand, two hundred and twelve years after the birth of our Lord. I have seen my children and my children's children live and then die, yet I remain. Maybe the Good Christians are right and this visible world is evil, and so my living in it for so many years is just punishment for the compromises that I once made.

I write this in my own hand so that none other may be blamed. There are few now who might look for signs of the old heresy, but there may be some. If the reader wonders at one of low birth being literate, I should tell him that it was here long ago, in this convent of Sainte Marie, where I first learned to read and write. The sisters who live here now know none of my history, and have taken me in as an act of charity. They think my feeble health is due to my age, but I have decided to take that old route to the hereafter and eat almost no food and drink only water. Do I believe in those old forbidden rules? I am not sure.

I was born in the small hamlet of d'Eau, three miles from the larger village of Pite. The hamlet consisted of twenty cottages built around a spring. All the cottagers but one worked on the land owned by the great Count Raymond. My father was the exception, being a stone mason. He could have moved to a larger place but my mother was a nervous person and unwilling to leave her kin. My father's speciality was carving stone into statues of saints, and smaller items of alabaster, wonderfully wrought and which brought sufficient income for us to buy all that we needed, supplemented by my mother's vegetable garden. Some of the families in the hamlet followed the teachings of the Good Christians, a few even rejecting baptism for their babes. My family were at first good Catholics and I was baptised and taken to hear mass in the mother village. As I grew up and listened to the adults talking, I learned of the persecutions of the Good Christians, but none of it reached our small settlement and it all seemed far away. The people in both d'Eau and Pite lived and worked together amicably and although the elderly priest would press for a new babe to be received into the Church, he was for the most part happy for all to live as they would.

My mother's disposition had been brought about by the loss of all her children. I had had four little brothers born before me, who had all lived just a few months and were buried in the churchyard at Pite. Then when I was seven years old, my mother gave birth to a child, another boy who lived just a few hours. In her distress, my mother raved at the midwife who wanted to baptise the child, allowable in such an emergency. My poor mother had a madness come upon her and would let no-one touch the little body at first. My gentle father at last persuaded her to give up the child to him, but by then the priest had arrived, called by the midwife. On learning that the child was unbaptised, he told my grieving parents that he could not be laid to rest with his little brothers, but must be buried in unconsecrated ground with the outcasts from our people. When my father questioned him, the priest said it was God's will to take the child so quickly, and as for the burial, it was out of his hands. He, the priest, was under obedience and must keep the rules. At this my mother turned her face to the wall and would neither speak nor eat, and after three days my father and I were at the end of our resources.

One of my mother's friends who followed the teachings of the Good Christians saw my mother's condition and the next day she came, bringing a visitor. The leaders of the sect are called Parfait, or the women leaders, Parfaites. These live the holiest of lives, eating no flesh meat nor having carnal relations, but go about teaching, and labouring with their hands. The Parfaite sat with my mother. Maybe it was the novelty of having a woman in authority that reached my mother's disordered mind, or the gentle way in which she spoke. She said it was not God who had taken her child, but the evil god of this world. She said that he had been able to do this because my dead brother had been a perfect spirit and had not needed to stay long in the world, but could immediately taste the joys of heaven. She helped me bathe my mother, handling her with great care, and after helping her to dress in clean clothes, had prepared soup for us all, which my mother at last ate.

So my parents began in a small way to follow the way of the Good Christians. When my father asked if he should continue to make images for the church, the leaders said this was fine, as all material matters had no true meaning, and our lives continued as they had been, except we no longer walked to mass each Sunday. We sometimes had news of persecutions from the Parfaits who came to the hamlet, but all very far from our place and seemed not to affect us at all.

When I was twelve years old and able to understand more of such things, a great change occurred. Some of the fellow believers came to our house and talked long into the night. They said that the king of France had died and his mother queen Blanche was ruling, but this was a bad thing.

Then they talked about black friars and the 'dogs of God'. That night I dreamt of fierce black dogs chasing me and awoke from my sleep crying out. My mother came to me and I asked her who were the dogs of God? My mother comforted me and said they were not really dogs, but only friars, a kind of priest, who wore black clothes. I was not afraid of our elderly village priest and I tried to take comfort from my mother's words, but her face belied these words and in the candle light she looked afraid.

Soon after this the soldiers came. All were on foot except one who rode a great grey horse. The men were in the fields at their work, but my father came out and the mounted man spoke to him. He said that all the people in the hamlet must come down to Pite as soon as they heard the Angelus bell at noon the next day, and if they did not come they would all be judged heretics and the hamlet put to the fire. He shouted to the soldiers, who formed up in two lines behind him, and they departed, except for one soldier who turned back and struck my father hard with the hilt of his dagger, and my father fell to the ground.

I cleaned and dressed my father's wound and we spoke of what we should do. When the men returned from the fields they stood outside and talked in small groups. By the next day several of the hamlet families had left, but the rest of us walked down to Pite, to save our homes from being burned. At Pite we noticed many of the Good Christian families had gone. In all there were perhaps fifty people in the market square that noon, including a dozen children. There were more soldiers, outnumbering the village folk. The man on the great horse was there and with him two friars in black clothes. Our own priest was nowhere to be seen. There were also three covered waggons in the square, hitched to cart horses. One of the friars began to speak. He said that the foul heresy of the Good Christians, whom he called 'bougars' would lead us all to hell, and that if we knew of any who kept to this religion we must denounce them to him, and we would be saved. If we knew of them but did not tell, then our both our homes and ourselves would be put to the flames. We had but three days to comply. As he finished speaking the soldiers began to move and suddenly without warning they gathered up the children, myself included, and threw us into the carts. The screaming and wailing was terrifying, but so quickly and unexpectedly had this happened that there was little to be done. The horses must have been whipped up immediately, for the cart I was in, together with six other children, careered out of the village, onto the road and away. I was by far the oldest in the cart and I gathered the screaming children to me as best I could as we bounced along the road. Gradually the pace of the cart slowed, but the children continued to wail pitifully.

After some time that cart arrived at a convent. We climbed down from the cart and I saw that two soldiers had been with the driver. They shouted at us to be quiet and the children, the youngest of whom must have been about four years, were shocked into silence. I was old enough to be thankful that I was slight and of small stature for my age, with none of the physical attributes of womanhood, for I saw the evil look in the faces of those soldiers. I know now, though not fully then, what can be done by a mercenary army, bored with treating with a civilian population and a long way from home.

We were ushered into a barn full of hay bales, and the door was barred on the outside. I comforted the little ones as best I could, and the necessity of doing this enabled me to control my rising panic. After some time the bar was lifted and a lay sister entered and left some bread and a jar of water on the floor and then left and barred us in again. She didn't look at us or come near and I later learned this was because we may have been unbaptised.

For a day and a night we were kept in the barn, but the next day the door opened and a sister called me out. She was not dressed in the brown habit of the lay sister, but all in black except for a white linen head covering. I was taken to a large stone building and given some bread and cheese and a drink of thin ale. A basin was brought with water for me to wash and I was given a wooden comb for my hair. I was then taken into a room with a desk and a small shrine, with a cross and figures of the saints and a candle burning. I was left alone. I noticed a door at the other side of the room and through it walked a tall nun, clothed in black but wearing a jewelled cross which glinted with a red light.

She came forward and spoke. "You were baptised a true Christian. Do you understand the danger into which you have fallen?"

"I am only a child and must do as my elders say," I replied.

"A clever answer. But you are old enough to understand right from wrong, are you not?"

"Where are my parents? Can you tell me what has happened to them?"

"I do not know."

"Can you find this out? Can you tell me?"

She thought for a moment.

"I too am under obedience. We live under the rule of Saint Benedict and obey all those in authority over us. They in turn obey God."

I was always a clever child and had listened to the teachings of the Good Christians and knew which of the Catholic Church's tenets they disputed. *The rules*, I thought. *Know the rules. Always the rules that men teach.*

Suddenly a figure came through the doorway. The black friar from the village square.

"Enough!" he said. He looked at me and his eyes were fierce and bright. "You are a brand plucked from the burning! A child rescued from the hell that awaits those who follow the devil's path."

I fell to my knees and blessed myself with the sign of the cross.

"God be praised!" said the Reverend Mother. "See, Father, she can make the sign."

I was taken out and back into the barn, but all the children had gone. I was very afraid by now, but the next day I was given the rough brown habit of a lay sister to wear, my hair was cut short, and I was provided with a linen head cloth.

So began my first time living at this convent. I knew my survival depended on my behaviour and I stood with the lay sisters at the back of the chapel for the Offices, kept quiet, and worked hard at my tasks. At first I was used for the roughest work and to run errands, but Sister Christine who ran the infirmary took note of me, especially as in any free moment I liked to help with the sick. Gradually I spent more time there and was given permission to assist her. It was here that I first saw a book, for Christine was literate and wrote down her recipes for the cures she effected, using the herbs which she grew. I once had the courage to ask Christine if she knew of the fate of my parents, but she just turned away. So three years went past. I knew I could never enter the Order as I had no dowry, but I was glad of this. I kept quiet and played by the rules, but my conscience was my own.

The nunnery was built of stone, but the outbuildings were all made of the thin red bricks made in our part of the country. As well as teaching me to read, Sister Christine told me many other things, although she never mentioned my past life. She told me that in the town of Albi there was a great cathedral built of bricks, with a tower that soared to the sky, and that the land round the convent was the rich clay from which the bricks were made.

So it was that in my sixteenth year a company of brick makers made camp outside our walls. They were to stay for six months making bricks, and then building new outbuildings for our house. Of course we lay sisters had very little contact with them, but near the end of their time a young workman burned his hand very badly and Christine and I nursed him. He came to have his hand dressed for two weeks, and I think Christine knew I liked him, for she gave his care to me, and that hand continued to be bandaged again and again long after the burn had healed. I was young and so was he. I knew before they left that I was carrying his child and so when they left, I left with them into another part of our country. We were married, but I never told him my true history, only that I was an orphan taken in by the nuns.

I heard of terrible things that happened to the Good Christians, and now there are none left I think. My husband grew old and died and then so did my three children. So in the first year of King Philip the Fair, who now ruled instead of our own Count, I sold all I possessed and bought an ass and packed what was left and travelled back to Pite.

No one remembered me. I asked about the hamlet of d'Eau and they looked at me blankly, but when I mentioned a spring to the North they said, "Oh yes, the spring and the cistern. Even in the worst drought we get water there, God be praised."

So I went, and there was the spring, now flowing through a cistern for easy access. But no people, not even a mark to show where the cottages had been. I stayed in Pite with an elderly couple who took me in, glad not of me but of the donkey who could be hired for coin.

So they too died and the priest, learning I had lived at the convent, arranged for me to return there, all wondering at my great age. I do not take the sacrament at Easter, and may refuse the last rites, which would not be offered if they were to suspect for a moment that I am never sure which rules I should follow.

[Extract taken from an original manuscript found in the vaults of the Benedictine abbey of St Mary and translated from the medieval l'angue d'oc by Dr Phillipa Bond.]

1348 Survivors

Father Peter stepped out of the church door into the moonlight. White frost covered every surface and long icicles hung from the roof, sparkling like diamonds, matching the starry pricks of light that filled the darkened heavens.

Only Will Carpenter and Gil Smith had been to Christmas mass. Smith's wife and children never left the forge now and there *was* no one else.

The twentieth year of King Edward, and all had been prosperity and peace. The towns were full of merchandise and the countryside full of beasts and grain. Four years later and Father Peter had the cure of only five souls. The first year of the Great Pestilence forty of the hundred and twenty in the village had perished, screaming as the great swellings burst. Peter and Will alone had been sick but then recovered. They spent days burying the dead, including Will's wife and five children. Then a year ago, The Cough had come. The children had died first, then the old, until only the six of them were left – Peter, Will, and Gil Smith and his wife and their two children. Smith and his family were the poorest of the poor, not even a cottage to dwell in, but all sleeping together in the smoke-filled forge, they had not been touched.

Peter, gazing up at the icy beauty of the sky dotted with bright stars felt nothing. He knew it would be time to move away soon, for the grain was nearly spent and they had killed most of the beasts for meat.

Then he gasped. In the sky, on this night of all nights, a very bright star – and it was moving, diving across the blue-black night under the great white moon in a shining arc, with a tail of tiny sparkling stars and then, after a few minutes, was gone.

For the first time in four years Peter felt a stab of hope. Will, who now lived with him as a servant, called from the door of Peter's house, a few steps away from the church.

"Come in and eat, Father. The broth is hot and the ale is warmed."

"Anon, Will," replied Peter, and stepped back into the church. He picked up steel and flint from a niche and, lighting a candle, he went towards the altar to pray. Why and what was that star? He knelt.

He heard breathing, rapid breathing, and turning, saw a small figure in the doorway of the church. He went back and guided the figure into the moonlight. It was a boy with a face that was skeletal. The child trembled and stared at Peter with great blank, black eyes. Although the boy was a stranger, the priest knew what that gaunt look meant. Those few who survived the Pest looked thus for many weeks.

"Who are you?"

The child stared fixedly and then crumpled to the floor.

Peter carried the boy into his house and laid him on his bed. Gently he pulled back the boy's shirt; there, above the skin that thinly covered his ribs, could be seen the scars where the swelling had burst and healed. Peter went to a cupboard and took out a small flask and mixed a few drops from it into a cup of warmed ale. Will looked at him; questioning.

"Aqua Vitae," said Peter. "Very rare. A few drops may help him."

Gently, the rough hands of the carpenter lifted the boy up. Carefully Will wrapped him in sheepskin, and then

Peter spooned the liquid into the boy's mouth. He swallowed, coughed and opened his eyes. A little colour came into his face.

"Where are you from?" said Peter.

The boy's great black eyes filled with tears and he struggled to speak. "Painwick."

"God's bones!" Will swore. "Forgive me, Father. But that is ten mile away."

The men looked at the boy as the tears spilled over and rolled down his grimy cheeks. The boy struggled to speak,

"No one left," he said.

"Could it be," said Will, "that they're all gone?"

Peter led Will away from the boy and spoke quietly, "We must get there as soon as we can."

Will nodded. He didn't need to be told that not just wild beasts, but the dogs men kept, would eat what they could find in such deep winter.

"We can't take him back there," said Peter and then together they said, "Gil Smith."

The Smith's wife and her two sons took the boy into the warmth and smoke of the forge. The poorest of the poor maybe, but the plight of the boy opened their hearts. They and Peter and Will Carpenter had a reason now to live when so many had died.

The boy responded to their care. He told them his name was Sim and he was the son of a weaver.

Father Peter and Will put the dead of Painwick into the church for safe keeping, and when it thawed, went back to bury them. Then they and Gil Smith and his family with Sim packed all they could gather onto three asses and left their village to find other people and start life again.

1368

Gil Smith has a fine house built of brick adjoining a large forge. He employs three men to help him. The gentlefolk who survived the Plague were hard pressed to find workers to tend to their needs, and a good smith could not fail to thrive. No one asks why his youngest son is dark-eyed and his two oldest so fair – not at least in his goodwife's hearing. She is fierce in protecting her family. She holds her head high and wears a fur hood in winters and is chief amongst the matrons in the Church Guild of Saint Barbara.

Will Carpenter has done well too. He married again; a Miller's daughter reputed to have 20 marks for a dowry.

Father Peter has retired to an abbey where he says mass, helps with the sick, and on dark nights watches the sky.

1429 The Dominican Letter

(I have translated the following document directly from the original C15th French. I have modernised the spelling, and inserted punctuation.)

Year of our Lord 1429, eighth year of the reign of the infant King Henry, sovereign of England and France, feast of St Mary Magdalen, July22nd.

From your humble servant, Father Jean-Luc Amerie OP unto Her Grace Katherine, Queen of England, Princess of France, greetings.

Fear not, gracious lady, that this letter will fall into unfriendly hands. As Prior Superior of our Oxford house I cannot be touched by prying hands, nor can my intentions be questioned.

I live to serve only you, under God.

It is now five days since your brother, Charles, was crowned king of France at Reims. I was there, and saw the Maid, dressed in armour like a man, standing by your brother as he was anointed with the holy chrism. Sacrilege!

I deplore the duplicity of the Armagnacs that seeks to rob your infant son of the Holy crown of France. I say no more of what needs to be done, but say that I obeyed your command to discover about the Maid, and through the good offices of my Order was allowed time to question her.

She was brought before me in a private room of The Order's House in Reims. She was dressed in men's attire, though not with armour on this occasion. She is small of stature and not lean, but of solid bearing, indicating her peasant origins. She is literate enough to sign her name, I was told, and speaks clearly in French, though with the heavy accents of her native Voges. Her hair was cut short, and her face brown.

She made no curtesy to me, but stood before me without even a bow of the head, and looked into my eyes directly. This is not good in a maiden.

I spoke at once, "You claim to be led by God, my daughter, yet surely God would not have you dressed so unseemly? Will you now confess your sin unto me and be absolved?"

"Sir, I respect you as an Holy Friar, but I have no need of your absolution. I am in a State of Grace."

I was very shocked by this. I began to worry that I was in the presence of a demon, so I said, "Please will you bless yourself now, with the sign of the cross and repeat the Paternoster."

I felt sure she would not be able to do so, as devils cannot bear the Holy Sign, but to my surprise she blessed herself right readily and repeated the Lord's prayer in Latin. Not garbled as the ignorant do, but quite clearly. Then I bethought me that the Satan himself was once an angel of light.

I continued thus, "How is it that one so poor and unlearned seeks to lead the great ones, even the Princes of this world?"

I had to be careful of course, in what I said. The Dauphin had indeed been crowned as Charles VII, and I was a guest his Court. The Maid did not answer, so I spoke again, "How is it that one so lowly can order those put in authority?"

"Doth it not say in Our Lady's own song, 'He hath put down the mighty from their seat, and hath exalted the humble. Deposuit potentes de sede, et exaltavit humiles. Esurientes implevit bonis, et divites dimisit inanes.'"

I was shocked to hear the Holy Scriptures quoted by such as she. Someone had been raising her up, and educated her even to learning Latin. I remembered though, that when Our Lord was tempted of the Devil, the fiend himself quoted scripture to ensnare Him. I was not going to argue points of doctrine with one such as she.

I continued, "How do you know the will of God, and what it is that He requires of you?"

"When I was thirteen, I had a voice from God to help me to govern myself. The first time, I was terrified. The voice came to me about noon: it was summer, and I was in my father's garden… I saw it many times before I knew it was Saint Michael… He was not alone, but duly attended by heavenly angels… He told me Saint Catherine and Saint Margaret would come to me, and I must follow their counsel; that they were appointed to guide and counsel me in what I had to do, and that I must believe what they would tell me, for it was at our Lord's command."

I would have stopped her then, but she went on, "Many have tried to persuade me from my calling. When I came to Chinon, they dressed my Prince, now by God's grace our true King, in the clothes of a courtier, and sat another upon the princely throne. The angels guided me then, and I recognised the true King of France among the press…"

I held up my hand, and she stopped. Then a servant came and called for the Maid to go unto your brother, the King.

I requested one more interview with the Maid. I asked

her how she knew that God required the Dauphin, now King Charles, to lead all of France. I reminded her, my Gracious Queen, that you, his sister, were now a widow and in mourning. How you grieved for your fatherless son, and how mayhap his birth-right was the throne of France. I was circumspect, being, as I said, in the court of King Charles. I made no claims. She closed her eyes and seemed in a trance. Then she spoke, still with her eyes closed and her hands uplifted as if in prayer.

"Saint Michael is here. He speaks to me. I am told that Queen Catherine of England is the mother of a King, and will be the mother of Kings to come. Not though, kings of France, but kings of England."

I spent the next hours in prayer and contemplation. I thought how the Maid had raised the siege of Orleans and won the battle of Patay. Could it be that the might of Burgundy and England be in the gift of one such as she?

Well, we are in the hands of God. Before I return home, I shall travel to Burgundy, to the court of Duke Phillip, and will write to you from thence.

I am ever your servant and true friend.

Jean-Luc Amerie OP

1431 Voices

30th May 1431

It was always the voices. They came in different guises. Sometimes she *saw* them, clothed in the garb of nuns, or as angels in dazzling white, but the voices were always the same. They were sweet and gentle and spoke of peace; of clear waters pouring down verdant hills to the open sea. "Follow our instructions," the voices said, "and all will be well." When she asked their names, they said they were holy saints; Saint Margaret, Saint Elizabeth, and Saint Anne, the mother of the Virgin.

Now as she lay in this dark cell, the voices had fallen silent. Could she have been wrong? She had signed her confession, carefully printing her name as she had been shown – JEHANNE.

They came for her the next day, and she walked bravely to her death. She had no priest to comfort her. She asked for a crucifix, but they said, "No, you are the devil's child." As she neared the place, a man, poorly dressed but with eyes full of pity, made a rough cross by tying two sticks together with the laces pulled from his doublet. The crowd was silent. When the fire had burned down they all walked slowly away.

17th June 1431 Eltham Palace

In the Great Hall at Eltham had gathered the senior members of Henry VI's court. The place was hung with bright tapestries and cloths of Arras, and the side boards shone with golden plate. The bosses of the roof were adorned with bright crimson roses, symbol of the House of Lancaster. Upon the glazed tiles of the floor were spread rugs of woven wool and sheep skins, and there were smaller tables holding ewers of wine, and sweetmeats. All awaited the arrival of the boy king, Henry VI, crowned King of England. Plans were already being discussed for him to be crowned king of France. He would be the first English king to be so anointed, but first he must be informed of the glorious victory over the French, and the burning of the witch, Joan.

The king's physician and tutor, John Somerset, had talked privately with Richard Beauchamp, Earl of Warwick, Henry's chief governor.

"Mayhap His Grace should be told the good news privily," he had advised. Somerset was fearful that Henry might be sensitive to the idea of burning a heretic. The Earl of Warwick was not a patient man, and when Somerset explained, he was not sympathetic.

"God's cullions!" he had sworn. "In a few years the boy will be king in truth, as well as in name, and we all dependent on his governance. He won't become a man and a king by hiding behind your robes, sir."

John Somerset had reminded the Earl of what had happened the year before, when they had tried to introduce Henry to the noble and princely sport of hunting. When the stag was pierced, Somerset had watched the boy become rigid, and when they had come, as was customary, to smear his face with the blood of the kill, he had become hysterical. He had been carried stiff and screaming into his bedchamber, and had suffered weeks of broken sleep. Still Warwick had not agreed.

"I must speak plainly," he had said. "I trust this may go no further?"

Somerset nodded, and followed as the Earl beckoned him into a private chamber.

The Earl had continued, "This boy's grandfather took the crown by force of arms, and passed it down to another Lancaster. God knows how I've fought for this House at home and overseas. Never can I forget the bloody campaign in France and the glory of Agincourt. Now it is all within our grasp. Christ only knows what may happen if this boy fails us. There are too many who may think they could do better. York is loyal, but he's married to a Neville; great breeders all. They may have many sons."

He stopped suddenly, and turned towards Somerset. "I am afraid," he said, "his…" He stopped and, turning, walked quickly out of the chamber. Somerset knew. Knew of what this warrior Warwick would fear, when no threat of battle or other physical danger could cow him. Henry's paternal grandfather had been the triumphant and warlike Duke of Lancaster, and his father the hero of Agincourt. His maternal grandfather, though, had been Charles VI of France.

So, they all waited in the Hall at Eltham. There was a flourish of trumpets and the young king came in, and was led to a dais on which was a stool covered with cloth of gold. The assembled company bowed in curtesy, and then a herald came forward with a parchment. He knelt on one knee and looked at the king. Henry was a thin child, with light brown hair which fell to his shoulders. He was dressed in a robe of scarlet edged with miniver, and upon his head was a narrow gold coronal. His grey eyes looked large in his narrow, pale face. He nodded to the herald.

The report of the defeat of the French and the story

of the maid was read out in formal Latin, but the boy could understand. He had been well taught and delighted in his studies. As he listened to the charges that had brought about Joan's downfall, the king held up his hand. The herald stopped.

"Why were we not informed of this before she was tried?" said Henry.

There was no reply. Some of the courtiers began to whisper.

"Silence!" said Henry. "Who set the seal on her death?"

Warwick stepped forward. "Your Grace, it was your own Great Seal."

The boy stood up. "No!" he cried.

Warwick came forward to try and calm the king. The boy held himself erect.

"No, No, No!" he cried, stamping his foot. He looked round the hall, and saw his uncle, Humphrey of Gloucester.

"Did you know of it, Uncle Gloucester?"

Gloucester came forward.

"You are yet of tender years, Your Grace, please come…" he began.

But the young king had lost all control. He began to shout and stamp.

"No, No no!" He stepped down from the dais and began to run round the room, pushing his way through the assembled nobles.

Somerset and Warwick at last got hold of him, and managed to carry him shouting and thrashing out of the room, but not before he had barged into a table holding the ewers of wine and fine Venetian glass drinking vessels. The wine, a deep crimson, fell to the ground, landing on the sheepskin rug. The wine became a stain which spread slowly across the pure white wool.

1476 Anne Neville

Dear Dr Barker,

I enclose the transcript of the Anne Neville MS for your perusal. As it is going to the popular press, I have not only updated the spelling, but rendered it into twenty-first century English without, I hope, doing violence to the spirit of the memoir. I would value your feedback in this regard.

Anne dates her writing from 'the fifteenth year of King Edward IV'. That is 1476, so as a good Yorkist, she takes 1461 as the start of his reign.

The MS is currently held at the British Library, but they kindly made a photocopy of one page so you could have a taste of the original. I attach it here.

No doubt you will find the contents as poignant as I. She is obviously so happy at this time in her life, and we know only too well what tragedies were to follow.

Yours sincerely,

Denise E Legge

I, Anne, duchess of Gloucester, write this in the fifteenth year of King Edward, brother to my Lord and blessed of God. I am full of joy and give thanks to the Blessed Virgin and the Saints upon my knees thanking them for the graces they have given.

I am here at Middleham, so dear to my heart, with my Lord and husband and with the babe God has given us upon my breast. I dare not speak much of the troubles I have born.

Though only twenty years of age, I was once married to my enemy, son of the She-Wolf of France, and then, oh worst time of all, when he and my father were dead, imprisoned by my sister and her Clarence, who has the mind of a Devil. But my own true Lord did not forget me. He rescued me, and brought me home. He is now Lord not only of this place, but of all these Northern lands. Peace is upon the country under his brother the one true King. The King and Queen are blessed with many babes to continue their line, the old witless king is dead, and the She-Wolf gone back to France. Our poor England is at last God's own isle again.

It was when I was ten years old and walking in the privy garden at Middleham that I first met my Lord, he being then a few years older. I was allowed to go freely about, being the indulged youngest child and beloved by all, but only the close family, and servants about their tasks were allowed in this place. As I approached him I could see he was no servant being finely dressed. I thought he must be one of my father's henxmen, who came to live with us and be trained in knightly virtues by my father. I was angry that he should be here and spoke saying, "Who are you? What is your name?"

He just stared at me and didn't answer. I was very angry that he didn't speak nor uncover his head and bow in curtesy to me.

"Do you not know that I am the daughter of this place? Tell me your name, sirrah!"

The boy just looked at me. He was about my height and his hair was long, straight and black. His eyes caught mine; bright brown they were with green specks and lively with humour. I was fascinated, but even more angry.

"Tell me your name so that I may report your evil conduct to my father!" I said.

"Dickon," he said.

"You must make curtesy to me," I said, stamping my foot.

The boy looked at me, smiled and, taking off his hat, made a low bow. Then getting down on his knees and throwing out his hands said, "Forgive me, gentle lady of the rose garden." All the time with a smile upon his face. I knew he was teasing me and ran off very angry.

My father's henxmen dined each day in hall, sitting at the low tables, whilst my family sat above them at the high board. When all were seated, I looked for the boy but could not see him, but noticed an extra chair at the high board. The two trumpeters came in and played and all stood up and uncovered their heads, even my own father.

How amazed I was when the very boy I had met that day came in behind the trumpeters and all bowed to him!

I sat next to my sister Isabel and asked, "Who is this boy?"

"He's the King's youngest brother, Richard," she said. "Come to learn knightly skills from our father. He'll have trouble with that; see how small and weakly he looks. Proud and indulged too, as the youngest. His brother George is much bigger and more handsome."

My face flamed. What had I done? Upbraided the princely brother of the King? Would he tell my father and see me rebuked? I hardly touched my food, but when dinner was over and all processed out of the hall, with the greatest first and my father and our family behind, Richard turned his head, looked at me, and slowly winked his eye. I think it was from that moment that my heart was filled with love for him.

The young henxmen had not much leisure, but Richard, because of his nobility, had more, and he would sometimes come to the solar, where we ladies sat at our sewing or books and talk, and delight to amuse us with his wit. He then would come and talk only to me, which filled me with delight. My parents seem glad of this and so we went on. When the young men had a mock tourney after the Corpus Christi feast and all the household came on the green to watch, Richard took my kerchief as his favour and tied it to his helm.

My sister was to be wed to his wicked brother George, Duke of Clarence. That evil man bewitched my father to rebel against the true King and his brother, my own Richard, and I was full of grief. Before he left, Richard came to me.

"We are young," he said, "but I will remain true to you, whatever befall. I will make you my own wife."

From his pouch he took two gold rings and showed me that in them was wrought 'semper verum'. He put one on his small finger and said he would never take it off until we were wed. He said that if I was in trouble, I must write to him, or at great need send the ring.

So our troubles began. At the worst of time, the wicked Clarence held me prisoner. I found a true servant and sent to Richard, and he came. I heard him shouting through the place, but his wicked brother had dressed me as a kitchen maid and warned the servants not to let me leave, on pain of death. Richard began to search but he could not find me, but refusing to leave, asked for meat and drink. I put my ring into a manchet loaf and God be praised, he found it. Then he came down to where we laboured and took me away to be his bride. Clarence had opposed our match for me being so great an heiress and they would lose the money.

Richard said, "Keep your filthy coin. I have that which is above gold and jewels to be my wife."

So here I am in true happiness and look to see my babes grow strong and our family increase in this beloved castle of Middleham.

1501 Catherine

13th November in the year of our Lord 1501, and a deep frost has London in its grip. In a large room in the Bishop's Palace in Lambeth, the cold is not a problem. An upper room has a fireplace in which a heap of logs shines brightly, made more fragrant by the herbs that are also burning there. Sumptuous tapestries line the walls, and the great window is glazed with costly Venetian glass. Beneath this window, sitting on velvet cushions, six young women are putting the finishing touches to a great piece of embroidery. Baskets of silken thread of all colours, including those made of gold and silver, are scattered about. One young woman is giving instructions, for they are putting the finishing touches to this work which will cover her bridal bed. In two days' time she will be married.

The young woman has the rounded cheeks of the young, a soft mouth, and her grey eyes are lowered modestly to her work. She speaks gently to her companions. Underneath this gracious manner, though, is a core of steel, for she is the daughter of Queen Isabella of Castile, one of the greatest princesses of Europe. Her warrior mother has trained Catherine well. She has been betrothed to Arthur, Prince of Wales, since she was three years old, which is twelve years ago now. She left the beauty and warmth of the Alhambra palace in May, and has endured long days of travelling, including great storms round the Bay of Biscay. Arriving in England in September, she has been on show constantly to high and low, and not once has she shown weakness or murmured complaint.

The girls talk quietly in the Spanish language. The embroidered cloth had been finished months ago, and they are just correcting any faults, and adding embellishments. It is sewn on deep red linen with shining silks, and depicts the fruiting trees of Catherine's native Spain, and her new realm of England. Around the border of the cloth have been sewn the plants that produce the herbs and spices used for food, each depicted in gold or silver.

Catherine has known from a child that one day she will be Queen of England, when Arthur's father, King Henry VII, dies.

Suddenly she puts down her work and says in less than fluent English, "Now we will stop and talk the English I must learn and speak."

"Que Diremos?" one of the maidens says.

Catherine hold up a hand, "In the English!"

"What shall we say?"

Catherine thinks. "Nombraremos la fruta!"

For a few moments the sewing is forgotten, as they try to recall the English words for the fruits of the two countries. Mostly they can remember, but then Catherine looks at the depiction of a pomegranate tree heavy with red fruit.

"La Granada?"

No one seems to know the English word for this fruit from Southern Spain, but then their conversation is interrupted. The door at the end of the room is flung open and a ten-year old boy runs into the room. He is richly but carelessly dressed, his doublet unlaced, and with no covering on his head. His hair, hanging to his shoulders, gleams red-gold in the light from the window. Henry is unabashed by the presence of his future sister-in-law.

"I have some special visitors for you. They have come

to see how well I learn. They say my Latin is most wondrous."

Catherine smiles. She too is confident in Latin; it is the tongue she and her young husband-to-be have used to write to one another. Isabella of Spain has broken new ground, and has had her daughters educated with her sons.

"Et huc venietis," she says.

Henry calls out, "Come!"

Into the room come two men, both dressed alike in sober black garments, though the younger man's gown is richly furred at the collar. They approach Catherine and her ladies, uncover their heads, and bow deeply. The young man says under his breath, meaning only his companion to hear, "Hispaniam est missus inaurum."

Though she is young, Catherine is a child of the royal court, where sharp ears are of utmost importance. Spanish courtiers learn to guard their tongues. She says in English, "Sir, I must practice the English. I know I am a *jewel* who will be given to the jewel of England."

The young lawyer, whose name is Thomas More, blushes deeply. For a moment he struggles to speak, and then, "Forgive me, my lady. I had left my manners at home."

The older man speaks. "Master More has perhaps not heard, as I have, how the Queen, your mother, treasures learning, and invites we poor scholars to teach both her sons and her daughters."

He turns to his friend, "Remember Thomas, when you shall marry, to educate your girl children well."

Prince Henry is growing impatient. He doesn't like it when the attention of any company is not directed at him. He draws himself up.

"Princess Catherine of Spain, may I, Prince Henry of York, present to you two great men of learning, Master Desiderius Erasmus Roterodamus, and Master Thomas More, Lawyer."

"Ah!" exclaims Catherine. "Then you may help us." She points to the embroidered pomegranate. "La Granada, what she is called in English?"

Erasmus smiles. "My lady, we do not often see this fruit in England, but it is known as pomegranate. This is from the French pomme, or Latin pomum, meaning apple, and also the Latin granatum, which means 'having many grains'. It is full of seeds. It is maybe the most fruitful of fruit."

Nobody speaks for a moment. Catherine stands up.

"How do you say in English, *emblema?*"

"That is emblem, my lady."

Catherine claps her hands. "Then la fruta Granada is my emblem. I will be Queen. I will give England many seeds. I will give England the fruta of Espana; many sons!"

1545 The Sea

My name is Mary Marriott, and I have led a blessed and happy life, thanks be to God, although now, as I reach my three score and ten, I know not how longer I may have. I see the children of my daughter, Margaret, playing on the greensward at the front of our fine house, and am thankful. I have never seen the sea. Living in an inland county, I have no wish to – with a good reason.

I was born before the turn of the century, in 1490, the daughter of a prosperous miller, who gave me a good dowry. When I was twenty, Henry Marriott, a stone mason, went to see my father and so I was wed, and settled for life.

Later, when the King began to close the Holy Houses, he sold great parcels of monastery land cheaply to the gentry, and this was the making of our wealth, for now those gentlemen wanted fine stone houses and Henry could supply them. Soon he had three journeymen and six apprentices, and we too had a stone house with goodly outbuildings. We were careful not to try to ape the gentry, and so we were trusted and throve.

My daughter was born when I was twenty-one, but no more children came.

One day, I opened the side door which led into the courtyard, and a young man stood there. He was dressed in a shabby monk's habit, and although it looked clean, it was very thin.

"Have you any work I may do, Mistress? The abbot can no longer keep me, for he sees which way the wind is blowing."

He then fell in a swoon at my feet. The apprentices helped me carry him into the kitchen, where I gave him meat and drink, and he soon recovered. Could he be given work? He was slightly built and his hands were delicate. But then I had a thought.

"Can you read and write and reckon?"

"Aye, mistress, and in Latin and French as well as English."

Henry was an excellent mason, but the heaps of indentures, bills – all the written work entailed in the business – vexed him. I took this young monk, Walter, into Henry's study.

"I think I've found you some help," I said.

Walter was a quiet young man, but very efficient at helping my husband. And so it went on, went on well. But I dearly wanted a son, to have his father's name, and keep our enterprise for the next generation.

I was sitting in our garden one June afternoon, and suddenly Walter was beside me. He carried a leather pouch and from it he took a silver badge.

"It is from the Holy House at Walsingham, and shows our blessed Lady. Please have it and use in in your prayers."

Well, Our Lady heard me, for in the year of our Lord 1520 my son Henry, always known as Hal, was born.

That child was never still. He thrashed about in my belly for nine months, keeping me from sleep, and when born, was upon his feet and running about in another nine months. How glad I was that Margaret was older and could keep a hand on his leading strings. Even so, he fell into the duck pond, the pigs' swill and was found one day, at three years old, two miles towards the Banbury road, all alone and singing.

Hal was to be apprenticed to his father, but, as all could see, his greatest gift was working with wood. He was apprenticed to a carpenter, but soon outstripped his master in making chairs, joint stools, anything that was needed. He could carve intricate shapes and often went with Henry to a Great House, and ornamented their beds or tables and chairs.

But still he wanted to travel.

One day he arrived home with a companion, Thomas Holden, whom we had never met. The young man seemed to be a gentleman, but pleasant and respectful. Hal was as excited as I'd ever seen him in all his twenty-five years. After supper he took us into the hall, and opened a large wooden box. It contained a document with the Royal seal, a leather purse containing a pound in silver coins, and a livery tabard in the green and white colours of the house of Tudor, with a Tudor rose stitched upon the shoulder.

"I have been appointed ship's carpenter!" cried Hal, "and not just any ship. This one has seen thirty-three years' service, and never been beaten. It is the King's favourite, called for his little sister, Mary"

I didn't want him to go on the sea, even though he promised to bring me spices, jewels, and I don't know what from foreign parts.

Henry thought it was a wonderful opportunity. What Royal patronage might flow from it and help his business?

That night I talked to Walter, privily, and much agitated. I blessed the day when we had taken him in. He calmed me, and next day gave me another badge, common pewter this time.

"This is the patron saint of sailors, St Nicholas," he

said. "He will help you."

The day of Hal's departure came. He and Thomas Holden had a horse each, and a sumpter horse with all their possessions on its back. Waiting to say farewell at our door.

As Hal turned to me, a rook in a nearby wood gave a loud call. Suddenly Hal's horse skittered and he was thrown. We rushed to him, and he sat holding his arm.

"Three weeks in a splint, and no less if you ever want to use it again to any effect," the barber surgeon said sternly. Hal ground his teeth in despair, and Thomas Holden rode off alone.

Hal was wise enough to know he must not jeopardise his arm, but his mood was surly, even though we all told him there would be other journeys very soon.

A week later a letter came, addressed to Henry. It was from Thomas Holden's father to say his son was dead, along with five hundred others on the *Mary Rose,* when it sank to the bottom of the sea that night. Only thirty-five survived.

1552 Destruction

Father Edmund White stood in the nave of St Mary's church and tears coursed down his wrinkled cheeks. He was a soul in torment. He knew he was damned, and even if he sought repentance, who was there left to give him shrive and housel? He had bought long life at the price of his soul.

Spiritual pride had been his undoing. How proud he had been when as a boy the local priest had praised his commitment to study, and recommended him, although the son of a lowly blacksmith, to a life in the Church. He had even been proud of his humility. He had joined the Carthusian order, who live a life of holy contemplation and do not have an Abbot or Prior, but see themselves equal before the Lord.

It made him feel no better that he was one of so many who had signed the Act of Supremacy. He had perjured his soul. They had made him watch as his eighteen brothers of the Charterhouse were taken out to be hanged, taken down alive and butchered, their entrails burned. After fifteen years, he could never forget it. Even now he knew he would not have the courage to face such a death. The reward for his compliance, his weakness, was this Cure of Souls in a prosperous market town, and all he could think of was his unfitness.

"Cæcus autem si cæco ducatum præstet, ambo in foveam cadunt."* he muttered to himself.

Father Edmund was not alone in his church. Six strong young men were working. As he watched, one climbed a ladder and with a mattock, struck again and again at the carved wooden figure of Christ on the rood screen. It fell to the ground, and as it fell the man on the ladder called out,

"Sim, get rid of this will ye?"

Another of the men, who was pulling an embroidered cloth off the altar, picked up the figure. All the men were strong and muscular; muscles built up over weeks of this work. He walked with the carving, and standing before a stained-glass window, he raised and threw it with force through the glass. The glass shattered as the figure passed through it. The other men stopped, and then gave loud cheers.

Sim then went back to the altar cloth. Edmund knew it well. It had taken three years of work by the town's women, members of the guild of Saint Clare. It was intricately stitched with patterns of lilies and stars worked in blues and golds. Sim took and knife from his belt and began cutting through the cloth again and again.

"Hold hard," said another of the men, "I could do with a bit of that for a sheet."

Sim grinned. "You can have some after me."

He cut a strip off the cloth.

"I'm off to the jakes. This'll be just the thing to wipe my arse!"

One of the men went out and came in with another ladder. He looked at the walls, many of which were painted with religious images.

"Paint over, or scrape?" he said.

Sim, who seemed to be the leader of the group, said, "Who wasn't listening? We're under fiddly Ridley here. It's got to be scraped so they can't ever get it back. Whoreson hard work, but pays better than lime washing."

None of the workmen took any notice of Father

Edmund, but went about the work of destruction. One up a ladder was scraping the painted images off the walls, whilst four of the others did the same for the paintings lower down. Sim, having destroyed the altar cloth, went round the church with a hammer, smashing the images in the side chapels. Anything of value, such as the gilt cross from the altar, and offerings left by the statues, was flung into a large wicker basket in the nave.

The north door of the church opened and a stout woman, modestly but comfortably dressed, came down the aisle – Alys Foster, wife of the innkeeper. She took in the scene with one glance.

"Don't know if you lads ever eat, but there's a fat swine been on the spit since sun up, and ready to slice."

The men stopped work and came towards her.

"Anything better to drink than the horse piss you gave us on the yester?" said Sim.

The woman grinned at him and swatted at his arm as he walked past.

"Young pup," she said. "I brew the best ale in three counties and well you know it."

As soon as the men left the church, the woman's expression changed. She walked over to Edmund. She laid a hand on his arm.

"Have they been in the sacristy yet?"

"Not yet."

"Maybe there's something we can save?"

"It's all inventoried. Had to write it out myself, God help me."

"Let's look anyway."

Edmund and Alys looked at the array of vestments and vessels arranged on two oak trestles, in the room at the back of the church. This was a thriving parish, and over centuries, gifts from rich and poor had built up these treasures, including gold candlesticks, finely wrought pyxes and an elaborate gold chrismatory. The vestments had been lovingly sewed by generations of faithful women.

"Will it all go?" said Alys. "Just like the bloat king took all from the brothers and the nuns?"

"All. The cloth will be used as blankets, bandages, sheets. The metal melted down for gain."

Alys picked up a book from a pile at the end of the table.

"And this?"

"Look inside."

It was a psalter, exquisitely illuminated with images in bright colours, enhanced with gold.

"They will destroy them all. They think pictures and images are wicked. Do they lead you into idolatry, Alys?"

"Well, I am not learned, but I know the difference between the real thing and a picture."

She picked up another of the books and turned the pages until she came to an illuminated picture showing Mary as the queen of heaven.

"Now here is a picture of our Blessed Lady; very beautiful. I know not to bow down before it, but I bethink me, if this be so lovely how much lovelier when I see her in heaven."

She moved across to the other trestle and picked up a

narrow piece of embroidered cloth laid on top of the vestments.

"A maniple. Very old," said Edmund.

"Not so old." Alys stroked it lovingly. "I remember, as a little maid, watching my Granddam stitch this. She wrought it all, and finished it as her eyes failed her."

Alyse folded the maniple in half.

"Turn your back, Father."

He did so.

Alys swiftly unlaced her kirtle. Her coarse linen shirt was not a tight fit, and she put the maniple down inside her shirt, next to her skin and then re-laced the front of her clothes again.

Together Edmund and Alys left the church and walked toward the inn.

* From the Latin Vulgate Matthew 15 v 14 *If the blind lead the blind, both shall fall*

[Bibliography:
Primary Source
1. *The First Prayer Book of Edward V1*
Londini in Officina
Edourardi Whitchurche
Cum privilegio ad imprimendum solum
Anno Do. 1549 Mense Martii

Secondary Sources
1. *The Stripping of the Altars: Traditional Religion in England 1400-1580*
Eamon Duffy
Yale University Press 1992

2. *Voices of Morebath : Reformation & Rebellion in an English Village*
Eamon Duffy
Yale University Press 2001

3. *The Reformation Experience: Living through the turbulent C16th*
Eric Ives
Lion Hudson 2012

4. *The Monastic Estate*

Peter Clary - Phillimore Book Publishing 2015]

1571 Hugh Pedlar

Following the accession of Elizabeth I a third Act of Uniformity was passed in 1559, authorising a book of common prayer which was similar to the 1552 version, but which retained some Catholic elements. The Act required church attendance on Sundays and holy days and imposed fines for each day absent.

In February 1570, Pope Pius V declared that Elizabeth was a heretic. The Bull released Catholics from any loyalty to Elizabeth and called upon them to remove her from the throne.

***

Thomas Morris was a happy and yet unhappy man. Devout from a youth, he could not imagine how all the past, the reassuring habitual past, would be swept away. The parish church was the centre of his life as a child. It was a place of beauty, with two windows of stained glass, which his family had helped to buy a hundred years ago. The walls were painted with highly coloured stories from the gospels, 'good books for the unlearned', his father had told him. There was a carved and painted rood screen, with carvings of the saints and the Holy Rood atop it, and always the light of many candles. It was a place for the living and the remembered dead, as the anniversaries of those who had lived and died here were never forgotten.

Thomas knew it was time to tell his children the truth. He remembered the great fasts and greater feasts, and especially the Corpus Christi procession, for it was on one such day he had seen their mother, Anne, among the other maidens, dressed in white with flowers in their hair, and carrying a bough they had made, wrought with roses, accompanying the Sacrament around the parish. He was a skilled but lowly weaver, she the daughter of a rich cloth merchant, but he had won her. Her father had recognised Thomas's piety and also his willingness to work, and had taken him into the business, which had thrived. Their only sorrow was that no children had come, but despite the shrines having been taken away, Anne had kept a small image of Our Lady of Walsingham. When Anne thought her body was telling her that all hope had gone, her body had lied. Her courses had stopped because her prayers had been heard, and at the age of forty-five she had been brought to bed of twins, a boy and a girl, and by God's mercy all three of them had lived.

Thomas had seen the monasteries destroyed, and the lower gentry's loyalty bought by being offered great swathes of monastic land at cheap prices. All over England these men had grown rich and fat and would never relinquish it. Worse, much worse, was the reign of the boy king Edward VI. Their parish was under the jurisdiction of Bishop Ridley, the arch reformer. The stained glass was smashed and never replaced, making the church barren and cold, for the rood had been burnt, the walls scraped and whitewashed and the altar also burnt, along with the embroidered cloths generations of women had made. Under Edward there was just a plain table in the nave, but Elizabeth, at least, had allowed it to be moved to the east of the church once again.

Mary Tudor had given the Old Faith the final body blow, for the burning of so many had put fear into men's hearts, and every bare and barren church had, by law, its *Foxe's Book of Martyrs.*

1571, the twins, Mary and Edward, were now nine years old. From a young age they had been taught to say the Our Father and Hail Mary in English and Latin. Only three servants lived in the house, Oliver, a cousin, tutor to Edward and secretary to Thomas, and an older married couple, who acted as cook and housekeeper. When they dined at noon, with the door locked, these servants and the family prayed the Angelus before they sat down to eat. The children were told not to talk about their prayers to anyone; not anyone. They knew that their parents were always silent and sad when they went to church on Sunday, but four times a year, when the Communion was to be held, they stayed at home. The next day, the Minister would come to see their father, accompanied by the bailiff, and they could hear the Minister shouting, and father's gentle voice. Then mother would say "get out your pater noster beads and go and pray." It was all very mysterious.

The twins had always been puzzled by something else, but never had dared to ask. Curiosity was not encouraged, but now it was time for them to know. When Hugh the Pedlar came to their parish, he sold his wares for those who cared to come, and took his lowly meals at the inn, and travelled on foot as befitting an itinerant hawker. Before he left, however, he came to their house, but ate at the table with mother and father and Oliver, like an equal. Once they had crept down after being sent to bed and saw their Aunt and Uncle and two of their grown up cousins come into the house.

***

The twins sat in the parlour with their mother, and Oliver and Hugh Pedlar were there. Thomas told them all about the changes that the new religion had made, but how they believed the old, true Catholic faith. He told them the good and bad things that kings and queens had done, and then he said they could ask him any questions they liked.

Mary said, "Is the Queen bad or is she good?"

"She is a good lady, I think," said Thomas. "She has stopped anyone being burned for their faith, and also kept us from wars. We are able to trade and travel. We must pray for her."

Then Edward boldly said, "Why doth Hugh, a pedlar, dine with us?"

Then Hugh Pedlar brought to the table his pedlar's pack. He lifted the top tray off and underneath was another box, which he opened with a key. As he lifted things out of the box, he named them. An embroidered length of silk, a stole. Two small silver bottles, a cruet, to hold water and wine. A paten or small plate and a chalice.

He looked at Mary and Edward, "Tonight, I will hear your confession." Then "Don't look frightened, little Mary. I don't bite."

Mary smiled, "And tomorrow, Edward, you will help me serve mass."

1596 Midsummer Madness

It is June 1596. Why is the actor, Richard Burbage, sitting in the Stag Inn at Shoreditch, getting very drunk? He has a leather bottle filled with sack, and after every few gulps, calls for the inn's pot boy to fill a pewter pot he has next to him, with the inn's best ale, as a chaser. He is waiting to meet his fellow actor, Will Kempe.

Burbage and Kempe should have been happy men. They belonged to a company of players which two years ago had become so successful that they had been licensed to give performances at the court of Queen Elizabeth, as well as in the local playhouse in Shoreditch, which was simply known as 'The Theatre'. The Lord Chamberlain, Lord Hunsdon, who was in charge of all performances at court, as well as the censoring all public entertainments, had granted them a livery to wear, and the right to call themselves 'The Lord Chamberlain's Men'.

The Mayor and Aldermen of the city of London tended to be puritanical, and would like to have shut down this new form of entertainment, but with this official title, Burbage was safe. And they were making money; a lot of money. Burbage had begun to have dreams of building his own theatre on the south side of the Thames, Bankside, to rival Philip Henslowe's theatre, 'The Rose'. Bankside was free of the jurisdiction of the City Fathers and their 'holier than thou' attitude.

Public playhouses, being an innovation, had to commission new works, but Burbage had struck gold. One of his players, William Shakespeare, who was also a shareholder in the Company, turned out to have a gift for using old stories, from wherever he could find them, and turning them into plays which were wildly popular. By 1596 eight of his plays had been performed – parts one, two and three of *Henry VI*, *The Taming of the Shrew*, *Two Gentlemen of Verona*, *Titus Andronicus*, *Richard III* and *The Comedy of Errors*.

For the history plays, Shakespeare used Holinshed's chronicles, and although not a university man, the classical education he received at Stratford Grammar school proved invaluable. Thus his *Titus* was courtesy of Ovid's *Metamorphoses* and Seneca's *Thyestes*. Shakespeare used three sources for *The Comedy of Errors* – two plays by Plautus and part of a medieval play *Appollonius of Tyre*. There are many possible sources for *Two Gentlemen of Verona*, including Chaucer's *The Knight's Tale*. For *The Taming of the Shrew*, there were many folk tales to draw on and also one anonymous tale in verse *Here Begynneth a Merry Jest of a Shrewde and Curste Wyfe*, published in 1550.

With all this material, it was Shakespeare's genius to write plays which combined superlative flowing verse with witty and sometimes ribald prose. There was something for everyone, from the gentlemen who had seats upon the stage itself, to the groundlings who came in for one penny and experienced two hours of delicious horror, ladies fainting during *Titus* or weeping for the murdered princes, or with everyone collapsing in laughter at the broadest comedy. For this comedy there was no one who could equal Will Kempe and he had been secured for the Company by granting him a shareholding, so that he too was making good money. Who could ever forget his playing of the clown Launce in *Two Gentlemen* and, of course, his animal side-kick, the dog, Crab. It was rumoured that Philip Henslowe had offered a gold sovereign to acquire the animal for his company, *The Admiral's Men.*

But this evening, Richard Burbage was in despair. As soon as Will Kempe joined him, he called for the pot boy again, "Francis, Francis!"

"Anon, sir."

"Not anon, now!" roared Burbage. "Fill this bottle with sack and bring a jug of your best ale and a cup for my friend."

The pot boy scurried off to fulfil the order, and Will Kempe sat down and looked at his friend.

"Whatever ails thee, Dick?" he said to Burbage.

"It's Shakespeare," said Burbage. He groaned, and presented a piece of paper to Kempe, saying, "I don't believe it. I just don't believe it!"

"What is it?"

"It's the outline for the next play, and he has lost his mind!"

He pushed the paper towards Kempe, who said, "Just tell me."

"Well," said Burbage. "He has made this one up out of his own head." He groaned again.

"Tell me. Is it a history with kings and fights?"

"No," said Burbage. "No kings, no fights, no threats, no ravishing, nor calumny of any kind."

"A comedy then?" asked Kempe. "There must be a part for me."

"Listen," said Burbage. "It is a play with *six* clowns, ordinary working men, carpenters and the like, and they have half the play to themselves, because the story is they *themselves* are putting on a play. He wants us to see them *rehearsing* their play and then playing their play in the actual play; a play within a play."

"It'll never work," said Kempe. "I just can't see how this will tickle the crowd at all. Watching a play in a play. Have you tried to talk to Shakespeare about it?"

"You know what he's like, Will. He's gone to ground and no one knows where he is. He wants me to call for actors and all be here in The Stag next Monday. He's taken the upper room. But you haven't heard the worst of it yet."

"God's cullions!" swore Kempe. "There's more?"

"I can hardly bring myself to say it," said Burbage. He took a long pull on the sack, and put his head in his hands.

"Say it!"

"*Fairies*, eight fairies, with the king and queen of the fairies having the main parts."

"You don't mean it. Where are we to get fairies? What in God's name will they wear?"

Kempe pulled the bottle of sack over, and drank deeply.

"This might be the end," he said, "and we could have been made men."

How wrong they were. 'The Dream' was a great success and Shakespeare wrote another thirty plays. Burbage got his playhouse on Bankside. It was, and is, The Globe.

1611 A Great Opportunity

"Teach me the letters."

As long as he could remember, Ned Smollett had loved words. His father was an ostler at the Tabard inn at Southwark. Ned's mother had died giving birth to him and the shareholders of the inn, in pity, had let Ned stay with his father. All sorts of people, high and low, stayed at the inn; some petted him, some kicked him out of the way. He had learned to make himself useful – and he listened. He could mimic a young fantastic with a double ruff and cross garters, or the French gentilhommes, or any of the foreigners who flocked to London. At eight years old…he learnt to read.

"What would scrubby pot boy want with book learning?" a customer said, but he left him his copy of *Hall's Chronicles* and never came back for it. After many hours the words began to make sense.

Then, in the church there was the great Bible and Foxe's *Acts and Monuments*, with its grisly woodcuts. Soon he could read almost anything that came his way, including the playbills. One day in the gentlemen's taproom he picked one off the floor and read, "The Tragical History of the Life and Death of Doctor Faustus by C H Marlowe, performed by the Admiral's Men at The Rose theatre."

"God's teeth, Alleyn!" said a gentleman. "The kitchen boy can read!"

"'Tis the spirit of the great Geoffrey himself hangs over this place, Will."

It was good for custom. The Tabard had been the inn where the famous Canterbury pilgrims had stayed. Everybody knew that. The gentlemen amused themselves by giving Ned bits and pieces to read and he encountered words in a new way. He didn't know that, in sport, they gave him poetry to read. All he knew that instead of marching along the words made music. Then he got into a playhouse.

It was like a drug; not just poetry, but actors playing out the stories of kings and queens he had read in Hall, and comedy that made his belly ache with laughing. He saw *The Jew of Malta*, the *Spanish Tragedy,* and *Faustus* at the Rose. He walked across the bridge to the Curtain, to see *Every Man in his Humour,* but best of all, he liked the plays of Master Shakespeare at the Globe. He soaked it up. He lived it all.

It couldn't last. Ben Haddock, the usher of the Globe, had had enough, because of course, Ned Smollett couldn't pay.

"A cuff on the head and a kick in the bum doesn't teach him," he said. "The little bleeder gets in again and again."

"How so?" said a colleague.

"Damned if I know. Under the skirts of our Lord Bishop's geese, I shouldn't wonder. But I'll have him. I'll learn him a lesson, he'll clear off for good."

Ned was at the front of the yard. If he stood on his rolled-up doublet, his eyes were level with the stage. A heavy hand, and he was hauled from the yard, but not this time let go. He was lifted up and then next thing he knew, he was in a wicker basket with the top tied down. He felt it being moved and then all was darkness. He struggled, it was no use.

Two hours later the Globe was emptying out.

"A pot of ale, Ben?"

"Wouldn't say nay."

There was a pause, "Christ's bones! I have forgot that

boy! He's in a basket in the properties."

Ben and his assistant looked at the boy. Eyes streaked and face filthy with rubbing.

Then someone came up.

"What's this? A stowaway?"

"Bloody boy, saving your pardon, sir. Keeps blagging."

"What have you got to say for yourself?" Ben gave Ned a cuff on the ear.

"I need to piss!"

Then Will threw back his head and laughed.

Ben looked aghast, "Christ alive, boy don't you know who this gentleman is? This is Master Shakespeare. What have you got to say to him?"

Ned looked up and said,

"The poet's eye, in fine frenzy rolling,
Doth glance from heaven to earth, from earth to heaven;
And as imagination bodies forth
The forms of things unknown, the poet's pen
Turns them to shapes and gives to airy nothing
A local habitation and a name."

"I know this boy who is stealing my lines," said Will. "It's Chaucer's heir from the Tabard."

Shakespeare took Ned's hand and they went off together. They went first to the privy and then through the streets of Southwark to an inn called the Spur. In an upstairs room men lounged about round a table loaded with food and jugs of ale.

"Eat all you want," said Will to Ned, and then, "Boys, I have found my Mamillius."

So it was that little Ned became an actor. Not only

could he remember lines easily, but he had no trouble copying in the accents of the court. As little Mamillius in *The Winter's Tale* at the Globe in that summer of 1611, he brought tears to the most manly eye, and the ladies sobbed openly. It brought them flocking to the Tabard, and with the pay he earned, Ned's father put enough by to marry again. Two years later the play was performed at court as part of the celebrations for Princess Elizabeth's marriage to the Elector Palatine.

Edward Alleyne, perhaps the greatest actor of the age, realised that his little namesake was more than just a mimic. When he came into his property and founded his college, he took Ned Smollett with him, completing the boy's education. Ned became a master there, but still occasionally was called upon to perform both in the school and in the playhouse.

It was just as well Ned's education had been assured, for in 1642 the playhouses closed for good. That magical era had ended. Did Ned ever play again? For nearly twenty years the public were starved of dramatic presentations, unless the rantings of the killers of Christmas count as such. However, it was said that a man called William Davenant was Will Shakespeare's bastard or at least his godson. Mr Davenant received a patent to open the Duke of York's theatre almost as soon as Charles II had landed. Not outdoors like the Globe and no more half-penny groundlings… but who is this elderly man playing Justice Shallow there in the first performance in two decades of Second Henry IV?

"Jesu, Jesu, dead! A' drew a good bow and dead!" None other than Edward Smollett.

December 1648 A Father's Love

The twenty eighth of December and a deep and biting cold. Icicles hang from the eaves, and water is solid in rivers, streams, and butts. The Thames is frozen, but there is no Frost Fair this year, for no-one is inclined to be merry. There are few who keep the twelve days of Christmas, for ice has entered the hearts of men and the frost there is deeper and more deadly than any the weather provides.

The Greyhound Inn at Maidenhead is shut for business. The servants have been sent home and the taverner and his wife are alone; alone that is except for the Prisoner, six soldiers, and two men in black. Two of the soldiers stand outside the inn with hauberks to impress upon all who come near to pass on by. Inside are two more soldiers standing before the great bedchamber. In that chamber, the Prisoner is trying to get dressed. He finds it difficult, not just because his hands are stiff from cold, but because he is still unused to dressing unaided.

The men in black are in the great parlour and the remaining soldiers are in the kitchen with the host and his wife. The kitchen is warm as a fire is lit and upon it a large pan is preparing hippocras, the spiced wine that usually signals Christmas cheer. A piece of beef is upon a spit before the fire and the scent of these preparations fills the room and seeps out into the house. The atmosphere in the kitchen, however, is as chilly as the weather.

The hostess says, "I would not keep a dog without a good fire and vittles to its belly, much less any Christian soul, whomsoever they be."

The troopers stand together in a corner, their faces turned away.

"Whomsoever they be," she says very loudly.

Her husband says nothing, but goes to the fire, turns the spit, and stirs the wine.

The two men in black ascend to the bedchamber and the soldiers move aside. The Prisoner is brought out. He carries a small wooden casket. As he follows the two men down, the soldiers following, he stumbles on the last step. Looking down, he sees that the latchet of his shoe has come unfastened. For a moment, no-one moves. The minutes pass, and finally the Prisoner puts the casket down on the floor and fastens his shoe.

The parlour is furnished with a long oaken table, a chair and several stools. There is a board and cupboard along a wall on which are items of pewter plate. It is bitingly cold.

The two men accompany the Prisoner into the room. The Prisoner sits. The soldiers wait outside. Suddenly the door opens and the hostess enters carrying a large wicker basket filled with logs, and behind comes her husband with a wooden tray, on which there is a jug and slices of beef, bread and cheese.

The hostess takes the basket to the fire and kneels down, whilst her husband places the food and drink on the table.

"'What is this?'" asks one of the men in black.

"A sea-coal fire and good vittles," says the woman.

"It is not necessary. Plain food alone will suffice."

The woman has struck steel and flint and the fire burns.

"No fire?" says the woman.

"I say no," says the man.

The woman, who is not young but well-built, pushes herself into a standing position and looks at the man.

"If your brother or sister be destitute of food and you give them not these things, what doth it profit; James two, verse fifteen."

The man in black says nothing, but the colour drains from his face.

"Inasmuch as ye have done it unto the least of these ye have done it unto me; Matthew thirty-five, verse thirty-eight," says the woman.

The men in black leave the room.

The woman smiles. She and her husband bow and leave the room. The Prisoner takes a cup and drinks some wine but eats nothing. He too smiles.

The sound of a coach is heard outside and a few minutes later the men in black return, accompanied by three children – a boy of fifteen, a girl a little younger, and a boy of eight. The girl is very pale and looks unwell. The Prisoner looks at the men in black.

"Leave us," he says.

The men do not move.

The Prisoner rises to his feet. He bows his head slightly and looking up in a softened tone says, "A few moments, I beg of you."

The men leave.

The Prisoner and the children sit at the table and eat and drink. The Prisoner eats little. The warmth and food bring colour back to the boys' faces. The girl remains very pale.

The Prisoner asks the children to kneel before him

and placing his hands on their heads, he blesses them. As they rise, the young boy suddenly throws himself into the Prisoner's arms. The Prisoner kisses him and lets him stay upon his lap.

The Prisoner asks the girl to open the casket and he gives them gifts – a book for the girl, and a ring for the older boy. He gives the younger boy a small leather pouch on a cord. The boy opens it. Inside is a silver badge in the form of a hart.

"This once belonged to one such as I am now," says the Prisoner.

The boy puts it round his neck..

The Prisoner speaks. "Tell your mother my love for her is constant and she is ever in my thoughts. Be obedient to her in all things. When you are able, give my blessing to your brothers and sisters. Pray always to Our Lord, and forgive your enemies, but do not trust any man without good cause. There are many who would seek your hurt."

He turns the young boy's face toward him, and holding it between his hands says, "Sweetheart, now they will cut off thy father's head. My child, heed what I say. They will cut off my head and perhaps make thee a king. But mark what I say. Thou must not be a king as long as thy brothers Charles and James do live; for they will cut off your brothers' heads when they can catch them, and cut off thy head too at the last, and therefore I charge you, do not be made a king by them"

The boy draws in his breath and cries out, "I will be torn to pieces first!"

The Prisoner smiles, but the young boy begins to

weep. The older boy starts to weep and so does the girl. The Prisoner stops smiling. Tears course silently down his cheeks.

A month later, January 30th 1649, Prisoner, Charles I is executed.

January 1649

In a large wood-panelled parlour stood three people; a man in his fifties, plainly dressed in black, though in woollen fabric of the best quality, his daughter, aged twenty-two, and Anne, his wife. The women wore green gowns of similar woollen weave, with deep white linen collars. It was a very cold January morning. The snow lay thick on the ground, and long icicles hung from the eaves, although the room was warm with a log fire burning in the large hearth. This was the home of the wealthy London mercer, John Mellor.

The older woman spoke. "I cannot go, Jack. I will not go."

The younger woman looked round at her mother. It was possibly the first time she had heard her address her husband by the diminutive of his name.

There was a silence. A woman servant came into the room and put a log on the fire, glanced at the three people, and quickly left the room.

The daughter spoke. "I will go. I will go with Papa."

"No, Margaret!" cried her mother.

"I am of age, and not afraid. I will go."

Anne Mellor took her daughter up to her bedroom. She opened a large chest which stood under the window, and reached deep within it. She brought out a waistcoat made of rich crimson cloth and lined with fur.

"It is lined with vair," said Anne, "the finest there is, and very warm. Wear it under your cloak. I will have Thomas grease your boots too."

Margaret looked at her mother and then kissed her. She knew Anne had loved fine things, pretty things, before she had married John Mellor. Margaret had also come to learn, as she grew older, that while deferring to her husband, and seeming to be submissive, Anne was, in spirit, the stronger of the two.

As a child, Margaret had thought her father strong, and as invincible as the ground on which they stood. His was the religion of Jean Calvin. The Geneva Bible, with its glosses on the perfidy of kings, had been open on the table before every meal. Not for John was the new Bible of King James, with its bishops and priests. 'Not of works lest any man should boast' was his favourite text. If any man was sure he was chosen of God, it was her father.

Then, as she grew older, she began to sense his doubt, and then came to realise it was not just doubt, but a gnawing fear that possessed him. He was a man in a trap. He could not earn his way to salvation, but was he indeed one of the chosen? Right living was a sign of the election to the Saints, but then John was often irritable, impatient; a frightened man. They set out, John, Margaret, and the servant, Thomas, who carried a satchel of food and a costrel of hot, spiced wine. Large flakes of snow filled the air, making the land and the sky as one; a bleached white world. The fresh snow squeaked beneath their feet, and its pall deadened the sounds around them. As they turned into The Strand, and then west towards Westminster, they joined a throng of other people all heading the same way. There were none of the noises that usually filled the air on the street. No shops were open, and no hawkers sang their wares. It was a silent crowd, in a town gripped by the weather and a common purpose.

As they walked along, Margaret slipped on a patch of ice, and reached out and caught her father's arm. As he held her to steady her, she realised that he was shaking. Surely, he couldn't be chilled already? She looked at his face. He had no colour, only a grey cast to his flesh and deep shadows under his eyes, like bruises.

"Thomas, some wine for my Father," and then, when he had had a drink, "We can go home. We can go home, now."

John looked at her and shook his head, but as they walked, he kept her arm in his.

A large crowd had gathered near a platform in front of the Banqueting Hall. The area in front of the platform was kept clear of people by a row of soldiers carrying pikes.

"Good day, brother John."

"Good day, brother Hugh," said John, turning to greet a small, dark man "This is my daughter, Margaret, and my servant, Thomas. Margaret, this is Master Hugh Peter. Brother Hugh is a great preacher and man of God."

"We are keeping the common people away from the platform," said Hugh. "The wicked man of blood will be allowed to speak. We cannot stop that, but the sheep may be easily moved by his words. Our enemy, the Devil, can quote scripture, and who knows what poisoned, honeyed abominations may be spoken to tempt the weak."

"So, you keep them back so they cannot hear his words?" said Margaret.

"Just so, my dear, but I know you and your father have not the itching ears of the ungodly. Come, I am to assist in this act of heaven's justice, and I can get you a place near to the dais. Your servant must stay back though."

As they went to follow Hugh Peter, Margaret turned back to Thomas.

"Stay near, don't leave," she whispered.

As Charles Stuart was led out onto the platform, the clouds parted, revealing a pale blue sky where a bright winter sun shone. The air was crystal clear and still. The crowd became absolutely silent. Charles spoke out that he had always desired the liberty of the people. Then he asked for a cap to be placed on his head, and then he turned and faced towards the place where Margaret and her father stood.

His voice rang out once more. "I go from a corruptible to an incorruptible crown; where no disturbance can be, no disturbance in the world."

Margaret felt her father tremble, and looking up into his face, saw him looking towards the king. Slow tears were running down his cheeks.

She heard the sound of the axe fall, and a great groan came from the assembled people.

As her father's knees buckled, she held onto him, and there was Thomas at his side, stopping him from falling into the melting snow.

1650 Loss

The scene is a well-appointed merchant's house on the outskirts of a town in the Midlands. A woman of middle years is reading by a fire in a large parlour, which is decorated with swags of evergreens around the chimney breast and on the window sills. On a table in the room is a jug of hot spiced wine, the scent of which fills the room. It is 26th December, St. Stephen's day. Outside the country is in the grip of a severe frost. In another room someone is playing, without a lot of skill, upon a recorder.

<u>Characters</u>

MARJORIE BURTON: wife of the mercer, Philip Burton

JANE BURTON: daughter, aged twelve years.

GILBERT GREENE: the local clergyman

***

The sound of someone banging on a door; it being opened. Footsteps approaching.

MARJORIE: Gooday unto you and welcome, Master Greene. I did not expect a visitor in such foul weather. Will you sit and take a cup of hippocras? It will warm you.

GILBERT: I come not here to dally, nor to take wine with you, Madame. *He hesitates.* Mayhap, though, I will take a little.

Sound of pouring wine

MARJORIE: What can I offer…

GILBERT: I must advise you, Madame. I seek to save souls in this parish.

The music stops and there is the sound of running light footsteps.

JANE: Mama! Mama! I can play it!

MARJORIE: Jane, we have a visitor. Make reverence to Mr Greene.

JANE: But mother, I can play all of *Angelus ad Virginum.* Can I play it for you, now… and for Mr Greene?

GILBERT: What, child?

JANE: It's a very old carol. Mama told me and we read where it comes in master Chaucer's book. It is *Angelus ad Virginum*.

GILBERT: What is this Papist nonsense the child talks of? Should she not be reading her Bible. This tattle about the Virgin is straight from the mouth of the foul Antichrist that is the so-called bishop of Rome.

MARJORIE: Not so, Mr Greene. It is just the Latin for the visit of the angel. Jane, please pick up the Bible I have just been reading. Read for us from the Gospel of Luke chapter one, verse twenty-six.

JANE: (reading) *and in the sixth month the angel Gabriel was sent from God unto a city of Galilee named Nazareth to a virgin espoused to a man named Joseph…* (she is interrupted)

GILBERT: Enough! Do you seek to oppose me? I have come here for the welfare of your soul. I hear carols, when for these two years these evil superstitions have been forbidden. I see this place hung about with Pagan Popish ornaments; everywhere I turn in this room I see leaves of green cut from the groves of the wicked. This is what the ignorant did to celebrate in this season. It is forbidden for your own good. And where are your husband and sons? I know they fought for that Man of Blood, Charles Stuart. But the Godly prevailed! See how the blasphemer was brought to the reckoning. Be warned by his fate. Madame, I advise you, nay, admonish you. Turn unto the Lord. You have not been to church these two Sundays. The souls of you and your daughter, the man servants and maid servants in your house also, have been put in hazard.

MARJORIE: I will answer you, Sir. I hung the house with green to cheer us in the depth of winter with God's good creation. The leaves hung thus may be pagan, or they may be Popish, but surely, they cannot be both. The Bishop of Rome can hardly be accused of being a pagan. I know not if my husband be alive or dead, for I have not heard from him for over a year. One of my sons, God willing, is with him. The other son died at Naseby. His body lies close by in our churchyard. We have not ventured to church because the frost being hard upon the ground these three weeks. I would spare my household from the cold.

GILBERT: I will not bandy words with you, nor hear your excuses. I am here to examine you and the child. You will not talk, but listen to me, and I will judge you by the answers you give.

MARJORIE: Sir, you have come into my home, and I make you welcome. I will, however, not be silent at my own fireside. Jane, my child, tell Master Greene what we think of the Holy Virgin, the Mother of Christ.

JANE: We always obey her.

GILBERT: Condemned! Condemned! Out of your own child's mouth. What further proof need I seek to judge this house, cast out from the fellowship of the faithful.

MARJORIE: Not so, Gilbert Greene. Know you what were the last words of the Virgin Mary recorded on Scripture?

GILBERT: Eh? Well...

MARJORIE: The last recorded words of Mary were at the wedding at Cana. Jane, pleased read to us from the gospel of John, chapter two and verse five.

JANE: (reading) *His mother saith unto the servants, Whatsoever He saith unto you, do it.*

MARY: So you see we obey her. In this house we try to obey

the commands of her Son.

GILBERT: Do you seek to teach me, Madame. Do you not know what power is invested in me? I can break you. Cast you and your spawn out from the habitation of the just into the outer darkness and to poverty.

MARJORIE: Have a care, Master Greene. This strife we suffer has divided us, but united some of us too. My husband and eldest son did indeed fight for the King. My youngest son died at Naseby, a hero for the cause of Parliament. Would you care to know also what was my name before I was wed? It was Bourchier, the name of the wife of Oliver Cromwell. Did you know that Elizabeth Cromwell has eleven brothers and sisters? I am one of them. Oliver Cromwell has forbidden music in Church, but I know he makes merry with music in his own house. Jane is practising her recorder and will play for him when we visit next month. He may be a man of war as occasion sees fit, but has compassion on his womenfolk, particularly when they are alone.

GILBERT: My dear Mistress Burton, and little Jane. I make no accusations. You must understand I seek only your good as your humble spiritual pastor…

MARJORIE: Good day to you, Master Greene. My steward will see you out.

Angelus ad Virginum was a familiar mid C14th carol. Chaucer mentions this early carol in *The Miller's Tale*, sung by Nicholas, the Clerk of Oxenford:-

> *And over all there lay a psaltery*
> *Whereon he made an evening's melody,*
> *Playing so sweetly that the chamber rang;*
> *And Angelus ad Virginum he sang.*

1651 Christmas Eve

It had snowed for a week, followed by three days of hard frost. That night though, there had been a mist, and when the sun arose, every tree in the woods looked as though it had been spread with a net of shimmering diamonds.

A child's voice broke the silence, "It's here, Thomas, it's here!"

The girl was ten years old, and dressed warmly in woollen clothes, topped by a hooded, fur-lined cloak of crimson. An old man dressed in clothes of plain green and brown followed her. He was carrying a ladder.

The child pointed to a patch in a young oak tree, and there was a bunch of mistletoe.

"I can climb to get it, Thomas. Just give me the knife."

Thomas had served Anne's father and his father before him and loved the family. He loved them enough to be firm when needed.

"No, Miss Anne, you certainly cannot. Be ready to get it when it falls."

Soon they were making their way back to the house, Anne excitedly carrying her basket of mistletoe.

"I can't think what the Mistress will say, with you out of the house before any fires be lit, and nobody broken their fast. You've put me back with all my work, Miss Anne."

He looked down at her and solemnly winked an eye.

"You'll have to say a word for me when we get back."

"Oh, mother won't mind, and this is the last thing we need to get. The parlour is full of holly and ivy in a heap. There's plenty to make a kissing ring and to put over the fireplace. Oh, how I love Christmas! We have the yule log already and mother says I'm old enough to drink from the wassail bowl."

"The food is enough for me. God bless your mother, but she keeps a bonny Christmas table."

The two walked back to the house, as the wood started coming to life. Birds called and flew, sending flurries of snow about their heads.

The manor was a large brick house, and fairly new, being built just as the old queen died in 1603. Under Elizabeth and then James, Anne's family had quietly managed to keep the traditions of the Old Faith. It was where their hearts were. They kept the Advent fast, although not the strict fast of their predecessors, but they did not eat flesh meat in Advent, so the goose and the boar and the many mince pies made Christmas a time of rejoicing.

Anne's father, Edward Weston, had fought for the King, but had been wounded in the shoulder at the very start, at Edgehill. He had been very ill, but survived, but with a useless right arm. He had two stewards, loyal capable men, together with whom he kept the manor and its lands well managed. So, life had seemed secure. All the tenants had known the family for years and there was a loyalty that went back through many generations.

Then they had cut off the King's head, and fear had crept into the house.

Thomas was soon busy making fires in all the rooms, firstly in the small parlour, then the hall. The house was not cold, despite the bitter weather, for the fires were left to burn and the bricks held the heat. There was frost on the windows, though, and Anne looked at the patterns made in the lattices. She traced the edges of the ferny frost on the glass with her finger, and thought about Christmas. There would be carols and dancing and she knew she was getting a new gown and sleeves. She had chosen the pink and silver fabric herself. Every thought was a delight to her today

Anne was a late child, born when her mother, Mary, was already a grandmother. Anne's older sister and brother, with their families, were arriving tomorrow to stay for all twelve days of Christmas.

The great hall table was never laid for breakfast, the servants brought ale and bread to the small parlour. But today there was something special. Gilbert, the cook, had called Anne into the kitchen and took an iron instrument off the wall.

"Wafers!" cried Anne, and soon her face was red, as she sat by the great fire and held the wafering iron over the heat. Then she turned the wafers onto a large wooden platter. They sat in the cosy parlour, Anne with her mother and father, and ate the wafers spread with butter and honey. There was milk for Anne and wine for her parents.

Theirs was an isolated parish, and despite the great changes in the country, had not been too affected. Edward had made sure his stewards kept him fully informed, but his injuries kept him from being involved in the war again. Not one of his tenants or servants had fought against the King, but they knew trouble would come to their peaceful lives now the King was dead.

They had just finished their breakfast, when Thomas came into the parlour.

He bowed to Edward Weston and said, "There are

men here to see you, sir, will you come?"

"No," said Edward. "Bring them here to us."

He picked a wafer and deftly buttered it with his left hand.

An old man in black, but warmly dressed with a hat trimmed with fur, came in together with a younger man, also in black, but with a starched white collar and a tall black hat. The older man took off his hat and bowed to Edward, the younger man did not.

The old man spoke, "They have taken the cure of souls in this parish away from me after forty years. I am to go."

"And not before time," said the younger man. "I am now your minister and will see that things are carried out in a godly manner."

Mary Weston spoke to the old man, "You know you have a home here if you need it."

"Thank you, my lady, but my sister is well housed and I go to her. But thank you for your generous Christmas gift. It has put my mind at rest, knowing I will not be a burden."

"Christmas!" shouted the younger man. "There will be no Christmas, none of the popery and gee-gaws of the past. That has all been swept away."

Edward looked at the two men, then spoke, "You have my permission to leave."

The older man left, the younger stood waiting, preparing to say more. All the family ignored him. He turned and left the room.

"These wafers are delicious," said Edward. "And I have decided our feast meat will be goose, stuffed with guinea fowl and a sucking piglet, and Thomas will find a coney or two for us. Now, Anne, you had better get the maids and start making that kissing ring.

"And Mary," turning to his wife, "have you organised the musicians for our carols and dance on St. Stephan's evening?"

Edward smiled to himself. It was good to be fighting again at last.

"I think I could manage one more wafer," he said.

1651 Again: Cecily's Story

Mother used to quote the Bible, 'in my Father's house there are many mansions', and although we secretly kept the old ways at home, we attended the parish church and listened patiently to our beliefs being condemned. This changed when father was killed at Naseby. She grew pale and quiet. Then we heard that they had chopped off the King's head. When my oldest brother, full of fury, left to fight, she grew quieter. They brought his body back from Worcester, saying all was lost, and the young King taken. Within a week, mother was dead too.

My brother, Henry and I were left alone in the manor, with only Murray, our old steward, and his wife Alys to help. The war had changed everything. The cousin, Richard came. My father would change the subject if his cousin was mentioned, but that September morning he and three of his servants rode into the yard. He walked through the house, picking things up and casting them aside, but when he walked into the chapel, he laughed.

"Oh! We have a nest of Papists!" he said, and then he and his men set about despoiling it, breaking and ripping all they could see.

Then Richard said, "A little horseflesh will cleanse this place," and they brought the horses, to stable them there.

Henry said, "I am the man of this house. Cousin you must stop this!"

"How old are you?" asked Richard.

"Fourteen."

Richard lunged forward, grabbed Henry's arm and said, "We'll see…you… young… whelp!" and with each word, slapped Henry hard on the face.

"Stop! You wicked beast!" I cried.

"What have we here?" said Richard, moving towards me. He put both arms round me and picked me off the ground and then flung me down.

"A little maid, indeed," he said with a leer. "I'd enjoy beating some manners into you. A nice leather belt, and get this brother of yours to watch."

We kept out of their way that first week. Murray did nothing to help. His wits seemed to have turned and he could only mumble. Alys couldn't do enough for Gilbert and his men, curtseying and bringing them wine from the cellar. Henry and I were alone.

Then a letter came for Richard. He called Henry and me and Alys to him.

"I am called away," he said. "I shall leave my man, Thomas, here to look after the place. Alys, keep a good watch on my two cousins."

After he had left, Alys spoke to Richard's man.

"Now, sir, how about some good sherris wine, I'm roasting a fresh fowl too."

Henry and I went to the desecrated chapel and tried to think. Murray came in.

"Quickly, you two. The wine Alys has given that devil should see him asleep for a day and a night. Come!"

We went down to the kitchen, where Alys was waiting, amazed at the change in her and Murray."

"We had to get behind their guard," said Murray. "They will talk freely before someone who they think has no wits, and Alys played her part right well, but we have to get you away. Richard wants this place and, with Henry out of the way, it will be his.'

We looked at him amazed.

"Oh yes," said Murray, "he plans a sudden deadly sickness for both of you."

Murray took us to the herb garden, and moving aside a rosemary bush, he lifted sods and took out a small chest. There was a pyx and pax from the chapel, some jewellery and money.

"You will take some gold, but hidden. Such as you are to become would never see gold coin."

For the rest of the day, Murray and Alys set about our transformation.

"They will be looking for a young gentleman and a lady, but they will not find them anywhere," they said.

All morning they had us moving and chopping wood and then Alys inspected our hands.

"Mmm, still a bit too clean around the nails. Do go and grub some weeds."

Henry had fairer hair than me, but soon it was darkened with walnut juice, which we rubbed a little onto our faces, and then our hair was cut off short to our scalps. We wore the coarse hempen shirts left by the servants, breeches and doublets and thick woollen hose and caps. Although I twelve and tall for my age, I am thin.

"Two labouring boys, by all that's holy!" exclaimed Alys.

"Now for your voices," said Murray.

We had spent enough time with servants to speak a good Sussex burr.

"If you are stopped, take my way. Play ignorant and

stupid," said Murray.

"But where are we to go, and how?" said Henry.

Murray put the chest from the garden onto the table and opening it, took out the silver pax. It was round and flat like a heavy coin with the figure of Our Lord on the front. He turned it over, and on the back a symbol had been scratched. It was like a rope folded over and secured by a knot, with a small crown inscribed above it.

"There are still many who fight in other ways than with arms," said Murray. "We keep counsel over the miles. The young King has not been taken. You will know what you need to know. Only show the pax if you have other assurances. He made us repeat certain phrases – " 'Are you not for the King? must get the reply, 'I am thrice times not.' If asked, 'Not summer or winter today, we must reply, 'Not until a green spring comes.' "

So we set off in the cart, loaded with casks of ale and barrels of salt pork, all covered with oil skin. Two humble brothers, Kit and Hal, heading for the coast at Brighthelmstone. We were to find the George Inn.

We covered miles the first day and all seemed well, but just past the village of Poynings, we met a small troop of horsemen. They were dressed in the buff jackets of the Parliament's men. The Captain spoke gently even though we seemed poor.

"We will take some vittles," he said, "But will pay. God rightly judges those who steal from the poor."

They rode off, singing psalms. I thought of mother. Many mansions.

We found the town and the inn. We tied up the horse

and, trembling with cold and fear, went inside. No friendly faces, but with sudden courage I went to the serving man.

"Not a summer or winter's day," I said in my roughest voice.

"God be praised," the reply came, and we were led upstairs to a chamber. We found a dark young man. We sailed with him on a ship called 'Surprise'. He had us under his protection, for our family's sacrifices to his cause. His name is Charles.

1653 Charles II

May 12th 1653, and the sun is glinting on the conical turrets and the moat which surrounds a small chateau ten miles north of Paris. It is nearly noon, and soon the Angelus bell will sound, and the chatelaine make sure all are gathered to pray, but not all will attend.

In a large room on the bel étage, the silken drapes are still drawn over the windows, and also round the tester bed that dominates the room. The bed is large but the feet of a man hang over the bottom edge; a tall man, then. The room is disordered. Various garments, drinking vessels, and broken meats litter the room. There are two doors, one a small one in the wall just left of the bed. A man enters through the main door. He speaks, "Monseigneur."

The young man in the bed sits up and pulls open the curtain. He is naked, and his long dark hair falls loosely round his shoulders. He shouts, "Allez-vous-en !"

The man hesitates, but from the bed a woman rolls, grabs a silken robe and leaves through the small door.

The servant speaks again, "Les messagers sont arrivés."

An hour later the same room has been set to rights, and the young man helped to wash and dress. An older man, soberly but richly dressed, enters the room, carrying a silver tray on which is a glass jug of wine and meat, bread, and cheese.

"Forgive me, your Majesty, but took I this from the servant at the door. I would serve you myself."

"By the Mass, Will Compton, you are welcome, doubly so as you talk English. Pour me some wine and tell me the news."

The man puts the tray on a small table, pours some wine, and moves over to the King's chair. He goes down on one knee.

"No need for that, Will. Get a chair and sit with me."

"But, my Lord…"

"I know. I know. My poor father insisted on being served so, but all is changed, by God. What am I but a poor cousin here, without two sous to bless myself. Tell me what goes forth in my poor benighted kingdom?"

"A man has come with news. I have brought him with me. He is lowly. Forgive me, very low, but loyal."

"William, William ! You have no need to teach me humility."

Charles stands up. He paces. In a moment he turns, his face anguished.

"By Christ, if it wasn't for the lower orders, the poor of England, I'd be in the grave along with my sire. I don't forget those weeks after Worcester. They succoured me, Will, like their own babe at risk to their lives. To be taken aiding me was their death. Not the clean axe, but half strangled and cut up, alive."

He pours some wine and drinks.

"But more than that, do you know what that demi-devil did?"

"My Lord?"

"He sought to buy them. Offered a thousand pounds for information. A thousand! More than a poor man would earn in ten lifetimes. Not one of them took it. Not one. None betrayed me."

"Your people love you, my Lord."

They both sit in silence for a moment. Then the King speaks.

"I don't forget. I don't forget."

After a while, Compton leaves and returns with an old man, very bent, and his hands gnarled with the gout of old age. He is dressed in plain brown cloth, but the linen at his throat and cuffs is very clean. He approaches the King and with difficulty kneels down. Charles moves forward to help him. The man suddenly reaches for Charles' hand, holds, and then kisses it. He begins to weep, the silent, tearless sobs of old age. Will Compton brings a chair and helps the old man to sit.

"I am a scrivener, sir, called in to serve, aged as I am, for those who are left in the parliament. The young go to fight. The old remember. I listen, I remember all. My body is old, four score and more, but my wits are true. I cannot stay in England now. I was born when the good old Queen was but a lass, but our poor England is sold, her greatness given over to the mob."

"Tell me."

The old man reaches into his doublet and pulls out a paper.

"These are the words the wicked tyrant spoke but a few weeks since."

He begins to read, "*It is high time for me to put an end to your sitting in this place, which you have dishonoured by your contempt of all virtue, and defiled by your practice of every vice. Ye are a factious crew, and enemies to all good government. Ye are a pack of mercenary wretches, and would like Esau sell your country for a mess of pottage, and like Judas betray your God for a few pieces of money. Is there a single virtue now remaining amongst you? Is there one vice you do not possess? Ye have no more religion than my horse…"*

The old man continues to read, and then there is silence.

Charles speaks, "Can this be true? Is the regicide himself to become as a king?"

Will Compton speaks, "I fear so, my Lord. The Rump has been…"

Charles begins to smile.

"You mean the arse has been well swived!"

They both begin to laugh, quietly at first, and then more and more, until they are wiping the tears from their eyes. The old man is taken away by a servant, and instructions given for his care. Later that evening, in a small room in the chateau, Sir William Compton and the King are alone. They have recovered from their levity of the afternoon, and are talking seriously.

Will Compton says, "There are many, so many like that poor scrivener, low born but loyal, and more from all conditions of life who want to see England restored and you, my liege on your rightful throne."

As Compton speaks, he toys with his silken sash, tying the ends into a knot. A sealed knot.

1851 A Great Invention

June 1851 and the area around the Seven Dials, near Covent Garden, bakes in the heat. The streets swarm with children, beggars and traders of all kinds, but in particular purveyors of second-hand clothing, known to the less educated as 'Slop Shops'. Mrs Bessy Baker is one such; a large and fierce middle-aged lady, known locally as Ma B, and the scourge of those trying to buy cheap, all thieves, and mischievous small boys. Ma B however, has a softened side to her nature, seen by only the very few. She is compassionate towards women in any kind of need.

Ma B's shop has rooms above it where she resides, but the top floor front is the home of the widow, Agnes Dean, and her daughters, Nancy and Nell, twelve and thirteen respectively. Ma B forgives them the rent. She tells Agnes that this is because the girls are such a help in washing, sorting and mending the clothes, that Old Sam the Rag Man brings to her each week.

"They are such quick learners," says Ma B. "They can spot real silk from shoddy any day of the week."

Agnes knows the girls work hard. She also knows Ma B could charge for the room, and she is grateful.

It is Saturday June 20th. Agnes and her daughters have scrubbed their room of any speck of dirt. There is very little else in it to clean. One bed, an old table and two stools, and a shelf with a few cups and plates and knives and spoons is the extent of their possessions. The girls are likewise clean and brushed in their well mended clothes and much patched boots, for today they are to have a holiday. Agnes gives Nancy a small hessian bag which contains a stone bottle, filled with cold tea, and a hunk of bread and cheese wrapped in a cabbage leaf to keep it cool.

At ten o'clock Old Sam is outside the shop and the girls climb onto his cart and they set off. They drive down the narrow streets and then into The Strand.

"Are your ladyships comfortable?" asks Sam, as they roll along behind his aged donkey. The girls giggle, but then become silent, awed by this new experience. They have never been this far from home before, nor travelled on anything other than their own legs. Sam boldly drives past Charing Cross, up The Mall, towards Buckingham Palace. Sam is not awed by anything: likewise his donkey.

When they drive past Green Park Nancy says, "Is this the country then?" She has never seen so much green in her life.

"Na. That's much bigger," says Sam.

When they get to the south east corner of Hyde Park, the cart stops.

"Look around," says Sam. "This is where I'll be. You'll know when to come back. All the swells will be leaving."

The girls get down. They know which way to go, for crowds of people are heading into the Park and they follow. After five minutes they stop. They forget the heat and their nerves or anything else at all, for there it is. The sun shines down on acres of peerless glass which reflects the light into and from the vast structure. Even on the sunniest day, Seven Dials is never really light; or clean. This is light that they could never have imagined. They stand and gaze and the crowds flow round them. They do not speak.

They know they cannot enter the building. Even the second-class price is half a crown on Saturdays and a shilling on weekdays. They do not need to go in. They want to look at the ladies.

Working with Ma B, the girls have learned to love and know the feel of fabric. When Sam has worked the streets around Regent Street and the Oxford road, there are often bits of fine stuff. They talk as they wash and then mend. They imagine what they would wear. Today, to add to the glory of the glass Palace, they can see whole gowns modelled for their delight.

The Crystal Palace is so large that the builders did not have to fell the elms that grew around, but built to contain them. There are, however, trees outside close to the building. The two girls walk round and find a large tree close to the First Class five-shilling entry gate. They silently eat their dinner, never taking their eyes off the glories that parade before them.

"Look at that pale pink silk," whispers Nancy, looking at the crinoline nearest to them. "It has little rose buds all round the bottom flounce."

"They look so lifelike," says her sister. The girls have never seen roses growing, but many for sale from flower women in the street, or in abundance at the wholesale stalls in Covent Garden.

"Her bonnet doesn't go, though," says Nancy. "I'd never wear pale blue and pink together." She becomes bolder, "It's a bit common."

"What would you have?" says Nell.

"I'd have ecru, with bands of pink velvet round the edge to match." She sighs with delight. "And a matching parasol."

Nell thinks for a while.

"It's that hot," she says, "I"d have white muslin with little strawberries stitched all over."

"And the parasol?" says Nancy.

Nell bathes in the luxury of unlimited choice.

"White," she says, "with a white silk fringe."

"Look," says Nancy, "by that man with the dog. A white silk parasol."

The girls stare in silence.

"And I'd have a sash," says Nell. "Strawberry pink velvet, to match the gown."

The whole day is passed thus. Their pleasure is complete.

It is still light when the crowds begin to stream away from the Palace. The girls stop on their way down to the road, to watch the ladies and gentlemen get into their carriages. Then they are on the cart with Old Sam and on the way home. They have no souvenirs. They have no money, but their delight and satisfaction is unmixed with any envy. If they could read, which they cannot, they may have read the words of a poet who died the year before.

Bliss was it in that dawn to be alive,
But to be young was very heaven.

1865 Eleanor's Story

I was born in 1865, the only child of a poor clergyman. My mother died when I was a child and so I became amanuensis, housekeeper, and sole companion to my father. Father was a learned but unworldly man. He educated me as he would have a son, and with my books, and my domestic and parish duties, my life was a not unhappy one. On the day the old Queen died, my father also left this world, leaving me a spinster of thirty-six, with no money and no home. Then I received a letter from the bishop of our diocese, asking me if I would be interested in taking the post of companion to the wealthy widow of a coal merchant, who lived in the nearby market town. I was relieved and thankful and together with my few possessions and my father's small collection of books, I moved into the home of Mrs Agnes Russell.

Mrs Russell was a woman large of figure, but small of intellect and imagination. Her only interests were her food, and reading literature of a narrow evangelical persuasion. I had a comfortable room in her house, and my work was not arduous, there being a large company of servants to do the domestic tasks. The remuneration was likewise generous, being a guinea a week, paid in monthly instalments. My role was to sit with Mrs Russell, read to her, and accompany her when she went out in her carriage. After six months of this life, I began to envy the very cook and housemaids their useful occupation. My only source of mental stimulation was the recourse to my father's books and the pianoforte.

Relief from this life of tedium came from Mrs Russell herself. Her widening girth meant she took little exercise and as winter came on, she developed a congestion of the lungs. Her doctor recommended a stay in a warm dry climate where the air was pure and fresh and she decided on a six week stay in a sanatorium in the Pyrenees. She would take only four servants; her personal maid, a groom, a footman to deal with the luggage, and myself as her companion. The packing and arrangement kept me busy for several weeks, but in early spring we set off, traveling by first class train to Dover and then by ferry to Calais. The journey exhausted Mrs Russell's small supply of strength and she slept for several hours, during which time I was free to wander and observe the people around me. Annie and Thomas the groom, I could see, were starting to form an attachment and happily went off together. John the footman was a respectable young man and was more than happy provide an escort for me. I was excited and stimulated by all I saw and particularly the freedom and gaiety I observed among Frenchwomen of all classes. From Calais we travelled to Paris, where Mrs Russell became unwell, and so began my great change of life. The hotel procured the services of an English doctor, who prescribed complete rest and the ministrations of a qualified nurse. For two weeks, we four servants were free to explore and experience Paris in the era of perhaps its greatest flowering. I had spent almost nothing of my six months' salary and so had funds to spare. Annie and Thomas went off alone and John agreed to accompany me. Now I am an old woman and have read all about La Belle Epoque, but then I experienced it new and at first-hand. In the parish of my girlhood there had been a retired schoolmistress, who had offered to teach me a little. Old-fashioned though it was, along with a fine copperplate hand, she had given me a grounding in the French language, which facilitated the awakening I experienced.

We went to Notre Dame Cathedral and La Madeleine and were amazed by their soaring beauty, and listened to the glorious music which poured from the organ. Only later did I realise that I was encountering the music of Saint-Saens, Fauré, Debussy, and Ravel. We wandered spellbound round the Louvre museum and imbibed the culture of the ages, awed at the artistry of the Masters of the Renaissance and Enlightenment. We discovered the small gem of Gothic architecture, La Sainte Chapelle. All round us was an air of carnival and freedom. I felt that I had lived my life in a small dark cave and suddenly had been transported into a wide world of kaleidoscopic colour. The whole city was in celebration after the Expositions of 1889 and 1900, with its Great tower and Galerie des Machines for all the people to enjoy, but there was more.

Together John and I explored the Seine and La Rive Gauche. The people seemed to live a life of holiday, with cafes on every pavement and everywhere musicians to keep them entertained. We encountered a new and revolutionary form of art. Along the river bank, artists set up their easels and we looked in wonder as they captured sunlight and shadow. As the evenings drew on, the people did not go home; the place became alive with light and the cafes and places of entertainment busier than ever. The artists from the streets came to talk, drink, and smoke. Daringly, John and I began to join them.

There was no need to introduce ourselves, for all were welcome, without ceremony. We stayed longer each afternoon at a favourite café. John had no French but I was able to tell him something of the conversation and soon the other patrons were calling, "What do you think, you quiet English?"

There was no distinction made of class or sex and no subject was taboo. They sketched continually and I have now, rather worn, a pencil sketch of me, made as I sat there one afternoon. It is signed Vuillard.

Mrs Russell's health improved and we moved on. New wonders awaited me. I marvelled at the great sculptures and jewel-like stained glass of the Cathedral at Chartres, and danced with villagers as they celebrated Shrove Tuesday with feasts and dances. Mrs Russell of course had no part in this, but somehow we managed to slip away on our journey south. Freedom and a lack of formality was the gift that Paris had given me and I grew closer to John. His father was a farrier and blacksmith in the Midlands, but John had longed to travel and had left his brother to take up that trade and gone into Service to see something of the world.

The Pyrenees worked a cure for Mrs Russell, but I dreaded a return to the stultifying life she led. I never received correspondence, but in the last week of our stay, a letter came for John. He came and found me and told me that his father wanted him to come home.

"He says the day of the horse is coming to an end. The new horseless carriage is the thing of the future and he wants me to study engineering and expand the business in that direction."

I stood silent engulfed by a creeping dread of my own future.

"Come with me, Nell."

I couldn't speak.

"I know I'm beneath you, but…"

I stared at him. Was this pity?

"I love you. There; I've said it."

I muttered something about age; he told me he was thirty-two. "What a child I am," and laughed.

As someone else has said, 'Reader I married him'.

We watched together, as a few years later the Great War wiped out the sunshine of those Paris days, but the use of the motor vehicle in that conflict made us prosperous. We are still together as the second World War comes to an end.

1889 USA

The child was very afraid. At first she had been afraid because she had disobeyed the rules and would be in trouble when she got home. Now her fear was mounting because she knew she was lost.

She was a child of these plains and had learned the ways of the West as she learned to speak. She had heard of Back East from her grand-parents; tales of crowded streets and many people and things bought for ready money, but the prairie was all she really knew.

She was a late child, born when her brothers were in their twenties and had amused the family when she was two years old by calling her two brothers 'Pa' when they had come back to help with the harvest. When her grandparents had claimed their land, there were no other people for miles around. Now, further along the creek was a settlement with a store, a church, and a school. The child was the first of her kin ever to have an education, but in this long summer recess, she was free to roam alone and barefoot under the vast skies. Pa had taken her boots, oiled them well, and put them in the barn until school began again after the end of summer.

The rules of prairie life. Never wander where you cannot see the line of trees that mark the creek, because you can follow the flow of the creek homeward. If going further, take one of the dogs. A dog was the key to survival. It could warn of thieves or worse on the long nights. Above all, a dog could follow a scent, so was a hunter of game, which on the long trek west had often been their only source of food. If the harvest failed, the prairie dweller still must hunt. More than that, the dog with his powerful nose could track mankind – thief or threat, a lost child or lost possession. It could find the way home. Every child was told the story of the farmer who had left his baby in a crib with the dog to guard it. On coming back he had found the dog and baby covered in blood and in his rage had killed the dog. Then he found the baby was unhurt and following a bloody trail found a wounded bear. The dog had fought off the bear and saved the life of the child, only to be killed for its pains.

The child had taken no dog, and many hours ago had lost her cotton prairie bonnet which protected her head from the burning sun. She knew that more dangerous than wild beast or native was nature itself. Heat, hunger, exhaustion, and above all thirst was the enemy of those lost in the wilderness.

It began to grow dark and her fear mounted further. She kept walking until she saw a line of trees. Not, alas, the rich growth along a river course, but the short scrubby growth that punctuated the open land. As she got nearer to the trees she saw a light. She approached carefully and then dropped down and crawled. There among the trees a fire had been lit and round it were a group of people. Some skins had been hung on sticks to make a primitive shelter and she could smell food. Indians. Suddenly there was a movement and she was grasped from behind by powerful arms, which wrapped her round, and her mouth was covered by a hard hand. The body stink of him was overpowering, but more so was her terror. Her heart raced, her bladder voided; panic engulfed her.

The Indian carried her and placed her down among the others round the fire. She immediately tried to get up and run. The iron hand grasped her and pulled her down. He spoke, "Stay, or I tie you."

Sitting round the fire were men and women not easily distinguishable in the gloom. A pot hung over the fire. Meat was cooking. Dogs wandered or lay amongst the people. The child remained still, rigid with fright.

A young dog broke from the group and came towards the child. It was not much more than a pup and it approached her with that lopsided, rolling gait universal in dogs whose tails are wagging too hard. It licked the child's hand. The familiarity of its presence broke through her panic. She reached out and stroked the dog, which rolled over at her feet. Her heart slowed and as it did so she became aware of a raging thirst. The Indian who had caught her reached into the pot with a gourd and offered her some meat. She shook her head.

"Drink," she said.

He went over to where a gathered skin hung on a stake and brought back the gourd filled with water. She drank. Then filling the gourd with meat from the pot he handed it to her.

"Eat."

She tried a little, picking with her fingers, and was surprised to find it good; fresh meat, not the salt pork which was the staple of home. She ate more.

Her panic subsided further. The Indians brought out a pipe which they handed round to one another. The meat and the tobacco smells further soothed her. The Indians had a wooden pipe; her father and brothers smoked from clay pipes, but the smell was the same, familiar and comforting. She remembered when she was very small being tormented by an earache. Pa had taken her on his knee and given her a suck on his pipe and she remembered no more of the pain.

Exhaustion took her and she slept.

It was the cold that woke her; biting cold from the ground. She sat up. There were no trees and no people. She was in open country and in the east, the sun was lighting the sky. She saw a movement and looking round she saw the pup from last night sitting alert with its nose in the air. She called to and it ran towards her and then stopped. Going to it she saw that it was tied with twine to a small stake. Looking in the dawn light she saw trees and a picket fence. It was her home. She untied the dog and together they ran towards the homestead.

1957 Freedom

"Darling, you can't possibly go out in that," said Camilla.

"Mummy, you promised. You said once I was of age, you would stop interfering."

"Angela, please listen to me for once. Just because you're legally of age, doesn't mean that Daddy and I have no responsibility for you. I can't have you going into town without hat and gloves. And really you ought not to wear red. With your Titian hair, you know the colour doesn't suit you. Where is that lovely green skirt and blouse I bought you last month? It would be just right for a fine day like today. You may borrow my best white gloves."

"I'm going just as I am."

"No, dear. You are not. You may be twenty-one, but remember you are financially dependent on Daddy and me. Not that we mind, of course. Didn't I ask Daddy to pay a year's subscription to the tennis club for you?"

"I hate tennis. I have no interest in tennis."

"So you say, dear. I really think you ought to join the club, though. You would meet all the right kind of young people. The right sort of young man. Mrs Ellis told me that her son Guy belongs, and he is going to be a solicitor."

"I earn my own money, Mother, and contribute to the household."

"Oh Angela, Angela, do you really think the little you earn as a clerk counts? Why you insisted on doing that clerical course night after night I never could understand. I had persuaded Daddy to pay for you to be properly Finished, but he took your part, as usual."

"Daddy understands."

"Spoils you, you mean. Richard has always been

hopeless, utterly hopeless. It took all my efforts to get him to agree to be take the Headship at Burlswood. Left to himself, I know he would have stayed at that ghastly Secondary Modern. Had some idea of doing good, I suppose. The only reason we can hold our heads up is because of the money Daddy's father left us."

"I've heard all this before, Mother. It's nonsense."

"How dare you talk to me like that? Your private school, the best clothes, all the things that give us some standing. It all costs money. Do you think, do you think for one minute, it comes from a Headmaster's salary, even a Headmaster at a school like Burswood?"

"Where does your money come from, Mother?"

"I don't think it is your place to ask me questions like that, Angela. Daddy had that inheritance from your Grandfather, that is all you need to know. You should be grateful."

"Are you grateful, Mummy?"

"You rude insolent girl. How dare you ask your mother a question like that?"

"Are you? Are you grateful?"

"Me? Grateful? It is you and your useless father who should be grateful. Do you think it has been easy for me? But I've kept our standards up; even when your father and I were first married, and I thought I'd have to live on his teacher's salary. And then there was you! That should never have happened. How he thought I was going to manage at home all day, alone and with no help! It is just as well for us that there was someone in the family who had some Background."

"Did Daddy discuss it with you?"

"Don't try to be insolent with your modern ideas. It is a man's duty to provide. Some man! Your father is weak, weak and hopeless. But I don't want to talk about this anymore. I'm starting one of my headaches. Please go upstairs and change out of those trousers and that nasty red shirt, and put on something I can be proud of."

"Mummy, I need to ask you one question."

"Oh dear. Make it quick, I need to lie down. One small question if you must, and then you can bring me up a cup of tea and a hankie soaked in my 4-7-11."

"Did Daddy actually tell you that Grandpa left you that money?"

"Of course. It was a month after his father died."

"Isn't that a bit soon to have gone through probate?"

"What? I don't understand."

"Mother sit down. Good. Now I'm an adult, and it is about time you became one."

"Oh! Oh! My poor head!"

"Does the word 'Littlewoods' mean anything to you?"

"No. Why should it?"

"Daddy's money didn't come from Grandpa or anyone else. He felt that when I was twenty-one, I had a right to know. Daddy's been doing the Pools since Littlewoods started in 1923. They tried to stop them during the war, but didn't succeed. The really good news was when they started the Treble Chance. He had a big win.

"I'm going out now. I don't think anyone else needs to know where our family got its money from, but you can give the green skirt and blouse to the jumble sale. Alec, my boyfriend, is a Teddy Boy and he likes me to look cool."

ABOUT THE AUTHOR

I have always had a fascination for the medieval and early modern period, and studied both the Renaissance and Reformation, and the works of William Shakespeare. I have also been involved in Living History re-enactment. I am particularly interested in the great changes the Reformation made in ordinary people's lives, and many of my stories reflect these upheavals. I intend to donate all the profits from the book to Médecins Sans Frontières.